THE COPPER HOUSE

JULIUS REGIS

A Detective Story

COPYRIGHT INFORMATION

Originally published in 1923.
Published by Wildside Press, LLC.
Visit us online at wildsidepress.com.

INTRODUCTION

KARL WURF

Julius Regis (1889–1925) was a Swedish writer and journalist from Stockholm. He worked in newspapers and publishing before moving into popular fiction. He also wrote about the new world of movies, which helps explain why his scenes feel quick and visual. Even when he wrote about complex crimes, he kept the language clear and the action moving.

Regis is best known for his detective character Maurice Wallion, a reporter nicknamed "the Problem Hunter." Wallion solves cases with sharp observation, steady logic, and a sense of how news travels through a city. Many stories begin with a simple report—a rumor, a brief note, a strange item in the paper—and then build into a puzzle that Wallion picks apart piece by piece.

His influences show up on the page. From the French side, there's a taste for bold twists and theatrical setups, like those found in Gaston Leroux. From the English side, there's the push for fair-play clues and a tidy wrap-up. Earlier adventure and science-minded writers—think Jules Verne and H. G. Wells—also left a mark on Regis's early work, which sometimes toyed with futuristic ideas before he settled into crime fiction.

In Swedish literature, Regis helped carry the modern detective novel to a wide audience. He wrote for everyday readers, not scholars, and valued pace, clarity, and fair puzzles. That mix—journalist's craft plus puzzle-making—puts him among the early builders of what later grew into a strong Scandinavian crime tradition.

Regis reached English readers in the early 1920s, and several Wallion adventures appeared in translation. These books tend to favor tight settings, odd hiding places, and careful end-of-story explanations. His career was short—he died young—but he covered a lot of ground across newspapers, novels, and film writing.

If you enjoy this style, there are other Regis titles worth seeking out. *No. 13 Toroni: A Mystery* offers a clean entry point to Wallion's method and shows how a simple clue can widen into a full case. *The Grey Guest* turns more personal, with pressure building as a hidden enemy closes in.

The House of Fire moves faster, with higher stakes and crisp chapter beats. Each gives a different angle on Wallion while keeping Regis's trademark speed and puzzle-first design.

Part I—The Whirlpool

PROLOGUE

This is the story of a great peril, and how it was averted.

It is surprising to think how few persons were aware of this peril, or had any suspicion of the extraordinary events that were taking place in Stockholm during the fateful year 1917.

Nevertheless, at the beginning of the year, a little weekly newspaper published a very striking open letter, entitled: "Who is the Man in the Whirlpool?"

To whom was it addressed? There was no indication, but the writer was evidently inspired by a deep and growing conviction of impending evil. The article ran as follows:

Have we lost all power of distinguishing between essentials and non-essentials? Stockholm has become a caravanserai, a link between East and West, a central clearing-house for all those who, under various disguises and with varying aims, seek to enrich themselves in the blood-stained arena of War. Can no one foresee what sort of crop must ultimately spring from this strife-sodden soil? It is tragic, while almost laughable, to see how people persist in labeling as 'espionage' every new development whose purpose is unintelligible to them, in the same way that they would probably account for all unexplained conflagrations with the glib verdict: 'a short-circuit.'

What *is* espionage? Of course, it exists. But is there nothing more?

Chips from many kinds of timber float on the surface of the whirlpool. What a medley of strange faces, which nobody recognizes, bob up from its mysterious depths!

The short-sighted public are content to go on believing that in Stockholm, where secret committees and conferences, planners and plotters from every quarter of the earth, are struggling together for the mastery, these dark deeds are one and all the work of secret agents of the belligerent powers.

Yet it is as certain as a problem of Euclid that at the vortex of the Whirlpool we shall find a group of intelligences working solely for their own interests. Let us suppose that amongst these, *one* alone is to be found who is strong enough to fight his way through chaos, or rather let us say, to *dominate* chaos. Would not such a man establish himself at the very heart of the Whirlpool, to direct the various powers of destruction whither he will?

We need not limit ourselves to supposition: *He exists*. We do not know who he is, and it is possible that his plans are known to no one besides himself. The air is full of rumors, and no one can tell what the future may bring forth. There is enough to show that a powerful will is evidently directing the activities of many of these lawless phenomena. Who is the Man in the Whirlpool?

Can no one answer the question before it is too late? For he certainly exists.

This appeal fell on deaf ears. The few who read it shook their heads, and laughed. The newspaper relapsed into silence with its next number.

To this very day, nobody knows who wrote the article, though Maurice Wallion can make a pretty shrewd guess. The article does not affect our story except as an example of the characteristic and frequently recurring collapse which precedes the fulfilment of a truth, as the prophetic slump gives warning of a financial crisis. It is known now that there *was* a Man in the Whirlpool, and in order to give an account of that daring adventurer's gigantic attempt to organize chaos, the author has had recourse to the evidence of a number of persons, in particular Messrs. Wallion and Raebel, and, above all, Mr. Leonard Grath.

But we must tell our tale methodically, and many things happened before the actual appearance of the arch-villain himself. The story opens, appropriately, with the arrival of two of the principal characters in Stockholm, that is to say, on July 19th, 1917. From that moment, the depths begin to seethe, the catastrophe looms nearer, and a Face appears amidst the foaming waters....

The curtain rises....

CHAPTER I

Baron Frederick Fayerling Waits in Vain
for the Most Important Document in Europe

"Well, what else?"

Baron Frederick Fayerling had a way of addressing his subordinates as though he were cracking a dog-whip. He was standing by his writing table, a strongly-built man of medium height, with cold blue eyes, and a beard in the style that D'Annunzio brought into fashion. As he looked down at the man who sat on a chair close by, he folded his arms, with a look of disgust, as though he were thinking: "What a face! The fellow is a regular freak."

The baron's well-kept teeth showed slightly, and the whip cracked again. "Next! The report on Tarraschin's memorandum."

The man on the chair, who was slowly and sullenly twisting his hat in his fingers, murmured in reply: "You forget, sir, that we are in a hotel bedroom, with all sorts of folk within earshot."

"And *you* forget, that when I wish to hear a report, you have only to obey my orders. What's wrong with a room in a hotel? Stockholm is absolutely full of spies and adventurers: so much the better for you—there is safety in numbers. Go ahead!" The fellow cringed to the lash, and made a start. "The man whom you expect is called Bernard Jenin," he said rapidly and softly. "I made his acquaintance, as you instructed me, and gained his confidence to a considerable extent. He is quite young and was traveling to Sweden by way of Finland, as we anticipated; I was his only companion in the north-bound train. I am absolutely convinced that he is in possession of the document: but he is cautious. I gathered that he is an ardent admirer of Kerensky, but as a matter of fact, he comes as a hunted fugitive from Russia."

"Did you manage to get a photograph of him?"

"Yes, easily: here it is."

Baron Fayerling took the snapshot and examined it closely. It showed a portion of the gangway outside a railway carriage; a man, wearing a very thin, almost ragged overcoat, was leaning against the iron railing, and gazing dreamily at the landscape through which he was passing; his clean-shaven face, with its broad brow and small mouth, was youthful-looking and attractive, but with a striking expression of calm resignation and patient expectation; his dark eyes were encircled by a network of very fine wrinkles, which might be the result of bodily suffering, or of many years of anxiety and strife.

"He looks weak," remarked the baron, throwing the photograph on one side. "It should not be difficult to—persuade him. Were you able to make any overtures to him?"

"No, he is not to be got at in that way; he is an honest revolutionary."

The baron laughed a little. "Honest? A dangerous attribute in these days of war! Where is he now?"

"As soon as Bernard Jenin and I arrived at Stockholm this morning, Rastakov took charge. Jenin believes that I am associated with his friends; I have no idea who his friends are, I never saw him speak to anybody or write a letter, but I persuaded him to engage a room in this hotel, and to await a visit from a common acquaintance, who will give him some important news."

"In this very hotel?" asked the baron sharply.

"Yes, he is at the present minute in room No. 23."

"Ah, in 23, that's better. Have you arranged that our friends should keep on the adjoining rooms?"

"Yes, all is in order."

Baron Fayerling nodded approvingly, and the man began to twirl his hat a little faster. His employer, who could read the signs of the times, smiled contemptuously, took out some banknotes and threw them down on the table.

"There you are!" said he. "One thing more: you have been in Finland since the beginning of January; what is your number there?"

"B.22," replied the man, gathering the notes together with a sort of enveloping maneuver.

"That is all right; in other words, we shall not require you here any longer."

B.22 rose obediently and went towards the door.

"Send Rastakov here!" was the baron's parting salutation.

The man disappeared, and two minutes later another person entered, closing the door quietly after him. He was a tall, dark, taciturn fellow, a regular Slav in appearance, about thirty years of age, with bold, resolute eyes, and a touch of self-satisfied impudence in his look.

The baron's expression had altered, and he now spoke in a frank, friendly tone.

"Good morning, Rastakov, did you meet B.22?"

"Yes."

"Did you verify his reports?"

"Yes, they are correct."

"Good; I don't trust the fellow any longer, and for the future he must be under supervision. Bernard Jenin is installed in room 23—with the most important paper in Europe in his possession, and now, Rastakov, the great thing is to get hold of it. If you are prepared to risk something for our cause, that paper should be in our hands in an hour's time."

Rastakov made no reply, but he tightened his thin lips with a look of determination.

"Have you warned all our friends?" inquired the baron.

"Yes, they will keep out of the way till it is done."

"And you have nothing about you which would compromise us, should you fail?"

"I am not a child!"

"Go in five minutes' time to Jenin's room, introduce yourself as the friend of whom B.22 spoke to him, and talk to him for a bit in such a way as not to arouse his suspicions, though he may feel a little puzzled. Then act as swiftly and silently as circumstances permit. I will give you a quarter of an hour. When you come out of the room, I shall be sitting in one of the wicker chairs near the staircase: you must pass me, and if you have the paper, bow slightly, and walk slowly out towards the Park, where I will join you in an hour's time."

The baron walked up to Rastakov, and looked meaningly at him: "If anything goes wrong, you must look out for yourself," he added: "you know our rules?"

"Yes," replied the other without flinching: "you need not remind me of them." And without another word, he left the room. The baron looked after him; his face resumed its usual cynical expression, and he laughed. "Poor fool!" he said half-aloud.

He looked at the clock: it was half-past twelve. He yawned, examined his finger-nails, and lighted a cigar. Then he took his coat, gloves and Panama hat, and went towards the door, which burst open as he approached it, and a short, stout, and very fashionably-dressed man came in. The two men stood staring at one another, without a word of greeting.

"Marcus Tassler," exclaimed the baron, impatiently, "what are you doing here? Be quick, I am in a hurry."

"Two minutes, only two minutes, baron," replied the new-comer, in an oily, businesslike voice. His flaccid sallow face, with its thick red lips, was as Jewish as his voice, but his hair was fair and close-cropped.

"I met Rastakov, and I know everything. But let me just warn you….."

"Warn me!" interrupted the baron, "it is too late for warnings. Our preparations are made, and must come to a head shortly; the Tarraschin memorandum will be the corner-stone of the edifice, and then the storm may break! If you are afraid, you had better be silent."

"No, I am not afraid."

"Well, what is it then?"

Marcus Tassler drew an opened telegram from an inner pocket and struck it with the palm of his hand. "I warn you," he said again emphatically. "This bomb business in Christiania has compromised our position, and there is danger in the air. Though no one may have discovered our plans, the Press are on the alert, and sniffing suspiciously in every direction...."

"Much that matters!" said the baron, coolly. "The fools believe that we are working for one of the belligerent powers, as spies and dynamiters: let them think so. The explosions in Christiania were a blunder, but nothing worse; the idiot who managed the affair, acted on his own initiative; I have isolated the consequences, and directed suspicion towards a quarter which will make the whole of Scandinavia gasp." The baron laughed contentedly. "We are stronger than any of the Great Powers, and our plan is the most colossal ever conceived by the brain of one man. So why need you worry?"

Marcus Tassler nodded, rubbed his hands, and burst out with a sort of enthusiastic eagerness: "Yes, I admit that Gabriel Ortiz...."

The baron shot a threatening glance at him: "Hush! Never that name, except in a whisper, or when you are alone."

"All right, our Chief, then. I admit that his genius seems able to surmount any obstacle: but, baron, his genius has not yet been put to positive proof. I am of opinion that what is just beginning...."

"Look here, are you ever coming to the point?"

"I begin to suspect that we have an antagonist."

"An antagonist? Are you mad? Since nobody knows us, how can anyone become our antagonist?"

"You think not? How about this wire from our Agent in Göteburg?"

"What does he say?"

"That Leonard Grath, the owner of the Copper House, arrived in Göteburg yesterday, and is already in Stockholm by this time."

The baron looked serious, took the telegram himself, and read it through.

"You can't think that this stripling will turn out to be our antagonist?" said he.

"No, but the fact of his arriving in Stockholm simultaneously with Jenin, points to a premeditated plan. You know what the Copper House means to us. No one expected that the owner would return, at any rate so suddenly. Do you think, baron, that someone has sent for him to turn us out of the house—that would be a catastrophe, wouldn't it?" The baron returned to the table, where he stood and meditated for a short time. "The Copper House—I didn't expect that news," he murmured, then turned round and said: "We shall find some way out of it. For the moment, Jenin is our chief consideration. Have you taken any steps towards having Leonard Grath met?"

"Yes, of course he is being shadowed, and the first thing to do will be to go through his papers."

"Right, and try to get me a photograph of him."

"I believe that has been seen to already."

"Presumably he will go down to the Copper House; that cannot be avoided, but of course he must discover nothing there."

"That is obvious!" replied Tassler. "But suppose he *should* find out anything?"

"In that case, he need not survive it. He might meet with an accident, the sea is close by—I leave it to you to work out the details."

As if by mutual consent, the two gentlemen avoided looking at each other at this moment.

"Was there anything else?" asked the baron.

"No."

"Then you had better go. We will meet at four this afternoon in the usual place. Don't come again to the hotel: Rastakov is in room 23 now."

Tassler's complexion looked paler than ever, and he did not wait to hear any more. When the baron turned round, he had left the room.

Baron Fayerling took a good pull at his cigar. The big hotel was very quiet, and the atmosphere felt close and lifeless under the heated sunblinds. Through the open windows he could hear the monotonous hum of the street, impregnated with the warm odor of sun-baked granite and asphalt, and punctuated by the crescendo and diminuendo of the trams, as they stopped, started, and rang their bells; in this third summer of the Great War one heard rather less of the hooting of motorcars, and of the groaning and creaking of cables, behind the smoke-stained walls of the central depot. The baron listened absently, whilst he bestowed another minute's thought on Tassler.

"They're a cowardly lot," he mused cynically. "Half of them are working to promote their own feeble ideals, the rest care only for piling up their banking-account, and they all imagine Ortiz to be an amiable idiot, whose shekels will further their own ambitions. Let them muddle along—the main thing is that we can make use of them."

He threw his cigar into the ash-tray, and his cold, calculating eyes glittered. "An amiable idiot? Why not? Time enough to decide about that—afterwards."

He left the room abruptly, closing the door behind him, and mounted the stairs to the next floor, stopping on the landing. To the right lay a red-carpeted corridor, similar to that in which his own room was situated, and just at the bend of the passage he could see a door numbered 23. This door, like all those near it, was shut, and the corridor was empty. At the top of the stairs was a sort of recess, with palms, three wicker armchairs, and a table with newspapers. In the chair nearest the banisters sat a gentleman reading one of the papers. The baron frowned: he would have preferred to find the place unoccupied; still, not the ghost of a sound was to be heard from No. 23, and with a comforting recollection of Rastakov's proved skill in transacting his business quietly and swiftly, he sat calmly down on one of the chairs, and resigned himself to wait. He cast a hasty glance at the reader, who appeared to be a middle-aged person, tall, powerfully built, and very well-dressed: his face was buried in the newspaper, and only the top of his sleek head could be seen.

Then the baron returned to his own meditations. He was surprised to find himself a little excited: do what he would, his eyes kept straying towards the closed door of room 23. The Tarraschin document would change the whole situation; its possession meant an increase of power, its loss, the renewal of such difficulties as are apt to wreck one's plans at the last moment. To be disappointed now, when everything was ready, and every day invaluable! Unthinkable, unless at great risk of an even greater disaster. Peace overtures were already in the air—who could tell, perhaps this very autumn…. The baron felt his excitement increasing, the suspense was beginning to tell on him: what could be the reason of Rastakov's delay! Perhaps Jenin had not the paper after all. And so many precious months had gone by already—what was the date?

The man reading the newspaper opposite to him looked over the top of it and said in a quiet, pleasant voice: "July 19th, 1917."

The baron started, and for a moment he wondered if he could have been thinking aloud; then he said stiffly: "Were you speaking to me, sir?"

"Yes," replied the other, as pleasantly as before, "I noticed that you were trying to make out the date of my newspaper, so I took the liberty of supplying you with the information."

The speaker had an intelligent, clean-shaven face, with aquiline features, and smiling gray eyes that beamed with a keen and irrepressible desire for information. Just now they were fixed on Baron Fayerling with a look which that aristocrat endeavored to return with equal self-possession.

He said hastily: "I am not aware, sir, that I asked you for any information."

The other smiled and answered slowly: "That is true, but I am delighted to overlook the—the lack of invitation."

The baron suspected a hidden sarcasm in his neighbor's voice or expression, but both were irreproachable. Confused by the situation in which he found himself, he colored hotly, and replied sourly: "Sir, you seem to me to be both persistent and inquisitive!" An instant later, he realized that he had forgotten himself; but the other man did not appear to notice what had been said: he struck a match, lighted a cigarette, and returned to his paper as though the baron had ceased to exist for him. The latter's self-control began to give way, and he stared mutely at the newspaper, behind which a thin column of smoke rose into the air. What business had the fellow on this landing? And would Rastakov never come out of the mysterious door of room 23? The silence seemed to become more intense with every moment that went by, and at last the baron could stand it no longer. He got up. The reader did not stir. He walked into the corridor and felt more comfortable now that he was out of the other man's sight. He passed No. 23, turned and walked past it again: not a sound to be heard. The quarter of an hour allotted to Rastakov had expired long ago. The baron looked all round him: not a human being was in sight. He put his ear to the key-hole: deep silence reigned inside the room. He turned the handle; the door was not locked. Finally, he decided to enter. On the floor in front of him lay a figure tied up like a parcel, with a handkerchief spread over the face. The baron lifted the handkerchief and saw Rastakov's bloodshot eyes glaring at him in dumb fury over a powerful gag. There was nobody else in the room.

A small envelope was sticking out of the prisoner's breast-pocket in a very obvious way, and the baron noticed his own name on it. Ripping it open, he took out a card, upon which a few lines were written in a bold, clear hand:

Dear baron—
    Bernard Jenin desires to be remembered to you, and I return Rastakov to you undamaged, having no further use for him.
                                                            Maurice Wallion.

The baron freed the captive, removing the gag, and cutting the cord into fragments. Rastakov sat up, but did not speak.

"Don't sit there, rubbing yourself like an ass!" exclaimed the baron. "What have you done?"

"Done?—nothing!" sputtered Rastakov.

"So I see. Speak out, man, what have you to say for yourself?"

Rastakov was like a madman: he beat his fists on the floor and shouted: "The devil take the room, and Jenin too! I came straight here, and nobody was about, except a man who was sitting by the staircase, reading the paper. I opened the door, and saw Jenin walking towards the window, and I saw nothing more, for somebody seized me by the arms from behind, threw me on the floor, and had muffled me up before I had the chance to get a sight of him. I am no weakling, but he must have been twice as strong. When he had bound and gagged me, he suddenly threw a cloth over my face, and immediately after I heard him whispering to Jenin. This lasted about a minute, then they left the room together, shutting the door after them."

"And Tarraschin's document?"

Rastakov made an expressive gesture, and the baron seemed to see the most important paper in Europe fluttering away into space, so near, and yet so far. The facts seemed to confirm Tassler's warning: "There are things which make me suspect that we have an antagonist," and as this dawned on him, he dragged Rastakov roughly up from the floor.

"Who is Maurice Wallion?" he demanded sharply. The other made no reply, and the baron rushed out of the room and along to the staircase. The mysterious newspaper reader was no longer there, but on the table lay an envelope similar to that which he had recently taken from Rastakov's pocket. The baron tore it open, and read:

"P.S.—I waited to see you in actual communication with room 23. I am indeed *persistent* when I have to deal with those who traffic in criminal mysteries, and *inquisitive* about abuses which I intend to expose. Maurice Wallion."

Baron Fayerling was no coward, but for a second even his blood ran cold, and he felt the first gusts of possible defeat moaning round him. But the blast subsided: he was himself again. Rastakov now joined him and he said to him: "Take the next train to the Copper House. I will telephone further orders this afternoon."

With these words, he too went his way.

CHAPTER II

A Young Man Arrives from California, and Hears Some Unexpected News

Mr. Burchardt the lawyer sat as stolidly as a grandfather clock beside his writing-table, and stared over his spectacles at Leonard Grath. It was an odd sort of reception for a lively young fellow who had just arrived from the other side of the globe, and Leonard Grath burst out laughing.

"What's wrong?" he inquired.

There was no harm in Leo, but he was young: to be quite accurate, twenty-six years of age. He was of medium height, well-made, with an honest, sunburnt face, merry blue eyes, brown hair, worn rather long as a tribute to his artistic propensities, and a large but sensitive mouth; to complete the description, he had the restless, flexible hands of an artist, a clear, confident voice, and just the least touch of foppishness in his appearance. The youth was no paragon; he was a happy-go-lucky fellow, not only in his artistic fancies, but in every detail of his daily life.

"Wrong?" echoed the lawyer, and a look of something like emotion flitted over his stolid features. "Things are no worse than they have been all along, but they are quite bad enough, Leo."

"Now for a homily!" muttered the young man, "and the title is: 'On the danger of getting into debt.'"

Mr. Burchardt looked pained.

"My dear Leo," said he, gravely, "you have not been much troubled with advice from me for some time: it must be quite six years since I last saw you. I suppose you remember that I have been the adviser of your family for the last thirty years. To all intents and purposes I have stood to you *in loco parentis*. Your only belongings are your Aunt Fernanda, her children and grandchildren in California, where you have stayed for so long that we began to wonder if you ever intended to come home...."

"Well, what of that? The Copper House couldn't run away from me."

"The Copper House *has* run away from you!" retorted the lawyer sharply. Leonard looked serious, and settled himself more firmly in his chair.

"That's impossible," he faltered.

"My letter concerned the Copper House," continued Mr. Burchardt. "I posted it to your address in Los Angeles, but you had already left. You have got home in the nick of time—for some things," he added, rather bitterly.

"I arrived in Sweden yesterday," said Leo. "I had a fancy to take a peep at the Copper House, and so I came over."

"And so you came over," echoed the lawyer, with a wry face. "It is a pity that the fancy did not seize you sooner. I fear that the Copper House is no longer yours, Leo, and that's the truth."

The young man colored up like a schoolboy, and said huskily: "Was that what your letter was about?"

"Yes, I wrote to request your consent to the sale of the Copper House."

"The Copper House for sale?"

"You may regard it as sold, my lad."

"What the devil do you mean?" cried Leo, springing up from his chair.

"What else can you expect, when a property has been neglected for three generations? Your grandfather spent the whole of his life abroad, and married in California, where he settled. When he died, Karka was mortgaged for half its value, although his sister worked herself to skin and bone in her efforts to reduce expenses. Your father certainly remained at home, but he entertained very lavishly, and his tobacco-growing hobby, which started very hopefully, proved a very costly failure. You inherited your grandfather's love of travel, and your idea of managing an estate apparently consists in telegraphing incessantly for money from the four quarters of the earth. During the last thirty years, I have warned first your father and then you how things were going. Then the War broke out, and now matters have come to a crisis. I can assure you, I have done my utmost to stave off the debts...."

Leo had been drumming on the window-pane, and now he turned round and said: "I know you have; I'm not trying to excuse myself."

The lawyer nodded, and continued in a slightly mollified tone: "I had not put up the property for sale, but at the end of March a purchaser appeared unexpectedly, and made a good—an uncommonly good offer, which we have no choice but to accept. I have drawn up the contract already and was only awaiting your consent to my signature, but since you are back, you can sign it yourself."

"My signature!" repeated the young man. He was filled with a sullen, boyish despair at the thought that, by a stroke of the pen, he must sign away the property which had been in his family for eight generations, and lose the old home which was the shrine of his childish memories.

"It can't be true, it's impossible!" he burst out.

The lawyer looked at him as though he were taking a careful inventory of the young man's weakness and lack of resource in this unforeseen emergency.

"Unfortunately it is only too possible," he said gently. The official atmosphere of Mr. Burchardt's private room began to irritate Leo like the touch of a hair shirt on a sensitive skin, and as the lawyer turned suggestively towards his deed-box, the young man said hastily, almost incoherently, as if attempting to stave off inevitable doom: "No, not yet! Give me a little time to get accustomed to the idea. I must have one more look at the Copper House whilst it is still mine...."

Burchardt looked thoughtful. Inwardly, he was deeply touched, but his severe expression remained unaltered, and he said to himself: "What a pity the scatter-brained fellow did not make a rich marriage, while there was time."

Aloud he remarked: "As you wish. But I have not told you everything yet. As you know, the Copper House, that is, the house itself, was let in the summer of 1915 to a person named Andrei Bernin. He is a Russian author, though I believe he has naturalized himself as a Swede, and he is living in the Copper House with his sister and his daughter. As regards the rest of the estate, and the woods, Suneson the bailiff continued to look after them, at any rate until last year; perhaps you remember him—a decent, trustworthy fellow. But he left the place very suddenly last autumn without giving notice. Andrei Bernin now rents the whole property, but the land is lying fallow. He's a strange sort of man—shuts himself up altogether in the Copper House; he seems to have plenty of money, and, not content with paying rent for the place, he has now made a very generous offer to buy it. I have never met him personally, as he is elderly and an invalid, and blind into the bargain; but I carry on negotiations with his friend and solicitor Marcus Tassler, who is managing the business with the most amazing energy...."

"Tassler," said Leo, with a slight grimace, "is he a German?"

"I should say he is of a sort of German-Russian-Jewish extraction, but all the same, he is a Swedish citizen," replied the pedantically-accurate Burchardt. "He is one of those financial experts who have come to the front during this War, and he is the Manager of the Finno-Russian Import and Export Company. Personally, I don't find him particularly congenial, but he certainly looks after his friend Bernin's interests with exemplary zeal. They have not allowed us much time to turn round; I have been obliged to give way a little here and there. A considerable sum of caution-money has been paid down already: if the sale does not go through, the lease holds good, and we are bound to undertake expensive repairs, whilst, over and above all that, we shall be held legally responsible for allowing the land to go out of cultivation...."

Leo turned quickly to the window; the truth seemed to dawn upon him for the first time, and he said: "I suppose the Copper House is filled with these people?"

"Yes, and all the old servants have left. We are absolutely powerless, Leo; the sale *must* take place!"

"Must it?" murmured Leo, still unconvinced. "Have you anything more to tell me?"

"Yes. Bernin, or, more correctly, Tassler acting for him, has bought up all the mortgages, and the largest outstanding debts on the property, and is bringing pressure to bear on us in that way."

Leo felt as though a net was closing round him: he was furious, and exclaimed: "The cheek of the fellow! So he threatens me, does he? I'll have something to say to him!"

"It is his way, I don't blame him. At any rate, we can't quarrel with the price he offers: it will cover all your family liabilities."

"Will there be any surplus?"

"About twelve thousand kroner, I should think."

"That isn't much," remarked Leo thoughtfully. His anger had evaporated, and he was smiling. "After all, I have always been hard-up, so there won't be a great difference. At any rate, the Copper House still belongs to me—nominally."

Burchardt came up to the young man and laid a hand on his shoulder. He had laid aside his official manner, and said kindly: "Take my advice, Leo. Life is hard on those who make no attempt to take it seriously, and we are living in an age when individuals as well as nations are being tested to the fullest extent of their capabilities. You are young, mentally and physically: that is one asset. You have had a good education: that is another. Face the future boldly, and win yourself a place in the sun: you *can* do it."

Leo looked at him: "Yes," said he, "that doesn't sound bad. But how am I to do it?"

"By working."

"Painting, do you mean?"

"I mean, by hard work."

"Chopping wood, perhaps?"

"By all means, if you are fit for nothing better."

The young man stretched his arms over his head, and laughed softly; then he began to walk up and down the room.

"I may be a ne'er-do-well, but I am not an invertebrate," said he. "I expected all this in a way, but I don't know how it is.... I feel somehow relieved. At any rate, I know now just how I stand. But," he added, with renewed vehemence, "the loss of the Copper House is an idea that it will take me some time to digest."

"It is too late to prevent it now, Leo."

"That is just what makes it so hard to bear! Besides, I can't get over the fact of such people as these taking such a fancy to the Copper House; I'm sure there's something wrong somewhere."

"There is nothing wrong with their money, at all events," remarked Burchardt patiently.

"Money!" snorted Leo, turning round. His expressive face lighted up, and he added eagerly: "Nobody knows yet that I am in Sweden. Suppose I go straight back to California, and try to make a fortune. How's that for an idea?"

The lawyer remained silent: he had not the heart to reply. But the young man's remark reminded him of something, and he bent down and took an envelope from his desk.

"Somebody seems to have expected your arrival," he said, "for this letter has been waiting for you since yesterday."

"A letter!" repeated Leo, taking it with surprise, "so it is, and by the postmark a local one, posted here in Stockholm. Isn't that odd!"

He opened and read it, first to himself, then aloud:

"Mr. Leonard Grath, c/o Burchardt & Co.,
Stockholm.

"Sir—

"Should you intend taking any steps with regard to the Copper House, may I beg you to wait for further information from me? The matter is serious. Above all, let nobody know that you are in Stockholm, and on no account go out to the Copper House. Ask Mr. Burchardt to observe similar precautions. He can tell you who I am.

"Yours in great haste,

"Maurice Wallion."

Leo read these lines once again. The lawyer pricked up his ears, as if at the sound of a bugle. "Maurice Wallion," he repeated.

"Yes, that's the name. What's all this about? Who is the fellow, and what does he mean?"

Burchardt took the letter, and read it in his turn, slowly and attentively. Leo, who was watching him, noticed that the lawyer actually looked disturbed, almost alarmed.

"What is it?" asked the young man, quickly. "Who on earth is Maurice Wallion?"

"Unexpected, perfectly unexpected!" murmured the lawyer. "Serious? Yes, that may well be, if *he* says so. Leo, this message comes from a man who wishes you well. I happen to know him; few persons have met him, but many have heard of him. They call him 'the problem-hunter,' and his nominal occupation is that of a contributor to the *Daily Courier*. But he is more than a journalist: he has a way of turning up on the scene of any crime or mystery, if he thinks there is anything abnormal about it."

Leo smiled slightly: "That sounds very mysterious," he said, "but as I am not guilty of any deeds of darkness, I can't say I feel particularly alarmed...."

"I was engaged on young Ravenscrone's case, when Wallion recovered his estate for him," replied the lawyer gravely; "that problem was a hundred years old: but he solved it in an hour."

"And now I suppose he will offer to recover mine," said Leo. "Why, what business is it of his? How did he know, to begin with, that I was coming here?"

"How, indeed," echoed the lawyer significantly.

They looked at one another, and the young man's smile gave place to a frown. "I call it either great cheek or a very poor joke for anyone to meddle unasked in my affairs," he said, taking up the letter to put it in his pocketbook.

Burchardt shook his head, and at the same moment Leo uttered a cry of vexation. "My pocket-book!" he exclaimed, "that scoundrel has stolen it!"

"Who has?" asked the lawyer, jumping up.

"A man who ran into me on the stairs about half an hour ago. It can have been no one else, for I had it in my hand not five minutes before. He was a tall, thin fellow, with black eyes; I thought he was drunk, for he barged right into me, without saying a word; I gave him a good shove, and he lurched out into the street. Of course the beggar was after my pocketbook."

"What had you in it?"

"Not much money, but practically all my papers, passport and everything."

At this minute the door opened, and one of Burchardt's clerks came in.

"A boy has just left this parcel for Mr. Grath," he said, putting down an oblong packet, and departing. Leo tore open the white paper, which bore no address, and looked up with a mixture of amusement and bewilderment in his face.

"What's the date today?" he inquired.

"July 19, 1917," replied the puzzled lawyer.

"Make a note of it, as being a day of surprises."

"What is it now?"

"I have got back my pocket-book. It is here, in this parcel."

"You don't say so! Empty, of course?"

"No," replied Leo, after looking through it, "that is the most surprising thing of all. Nothing is missing. He has not taken a single thing."

"Impossible, it's too absurd. Look again more carefully."

Both men examined the pocket-book again, but it was as Leo had stated: both money and papers were totally undisturbed.

"This is certainly a very striking commentary on our friend the 'problem-hunter's' letter," remarked the young man; "is he given to playing such tricks as these?"

"Nonsense," said Burchardt, curtly. "His letter is a warning, and this incident is a case in point. Some person has had recourse to an uncommonly daring way of finding out everything that concerns you, evidently wishing to identify you by the aid of your own papers."

In spite of himself, Leo began to feel rather uncomfortable but he pulled himself together, and said: "I begin to think that there is a general conspiracy to make a fool of me: a profiteering baron wants to compel me to sell the Copper House: a thief steals my papers, and sends them back untouched: a problem-hunter sends me unintelligible warnings—my poor brain is getting quite muddled! I wish I was back in California, there are such a peculiar lot of folk in Sweden, since last I was here."

"Listen to me, Leo," said the lawyer slowly. "There is something wrong about all this. That fellow Tassler must have some motive of which we know nothing. The first thing for you to do is to find out what Maurice Wallion knows."

"I am going straight to him."

"Now? He is not easy to get hold of, unless he wishes, but at any rate you can try."

"I intend to. So long, sir!"

Leonard Grath left the lawyer's office with his usual impetuosity, and ran whistling down the stairs. Burchardt's office was near the Kungstrad Park, and the young man crossed the road to get into the shade of the lime-trees. It was a beautiful, sunny morning, the beds were gay with flowers, and a great many people were about. A well-dressed man, carrying a small but expensive camera, passed him, turned quickly, and raised the camera; a click, and it was done. So rapid were the man's movements, that Leo did not at first realize that he himself had been the target of the camera. He took the cigarette from his mouth, and shouted: "I say, you there! You, sir!" But at that minute the unknown photographer boarded a passing tram and was whirled away.

"What next?" wondered Leo. "Another one who wants to know what I look like! I seem to be very much in demand!" He looked round him in perplexity and was presently aware of an uncanny feeling that he was being watched by someone in the crowd. Yet wherever he turned, he could see no one whom he knew, or who appeared to recognize him. Lights and shadows flickered through the green leaves, and the sunshine lighted up pretty faces and summer costumes. He began to feel dazed, and sat down on one of the green benches. "I must be dreaming," he thought. "This is all too strange to be true. Yes, of course I am dreaming."

He got up, walked on a short way, then stopped again. "If only I had the smallest idea what is up!" He laughed. "I shall go and see Wallion."

Ten minutes later he entered the offices of the *Daily Courier*, and asked for Maurice Wallion, half-expecting to be laughed at for his pains, and informed that no such person was known there. But the young and energetic reporter to whom he addressed his inquiries, looked at him attentively, and said: "Did you make an appointment to meet him here?"

"Not exactly."

"Then I'm afraid it is no use your waiting."

"But I have had a letter from him."

"Ah, that alters the case," observed the reporter, opening an engagement book. "What name, please?"

"Leonard Grath," replied the other in surprise.

"That's good!" said the reporter with a smile, immediately becoming much more friendly in his manner; "my name is Robert Lang, and you are expected."

"Expected!" echoed Leo, more astonished than ever.

"Yes, but I can tell you at once that nobody knows why, except Wallion. I am his assistant, and I believe he is most anxious to see you. Unfortunately he is out at present. I haven't seen him since yesterday evening, but step into his room, and we'll see."

They went into a small room leading off the corridor, and the cheery young reporter went briskly to the telephone. After ringing up several places, he said: "I can't get on to him, he is neither at his house, nor at any of the places where we can usually get word to him. It's always the way! Sometimes he disappears for weeks on end, and we can do nothing but wait until he thinks fit to turn up again."

Leo smiled, but he felt terribly disappointed.

"The worst of it is, that there is no time to lose," he remarked. "I fear it may be too late as it is."

"But you hinted that Wallion knows something about it already?"

"Yes, so I understand."

"Then you needn't worry. He won't let it be too late."

Robert Lang said this with a calm certainty that impressed Leo, whilst it made him feel more curious than ever.

"Do *you* know what your friend the Problem-hunter wants me for?"

"No, but that doesn't matter. I am only his assistant, his sub-lieutenant, so to speak...."

Here, the conversation was interrupted, as Robert Lang was called away. Leo wandered round the room, which was filled with bookcases, files of newspapers, and card-index cabinets. On the large writing table lay manuscripts, photographs, foreign newspapers, and several volumes of works of reference. The young man could see from a distance that one of the photographs was that of a charming girl, whose dark and rather appealing eyes seemed to be gazing right into his own. He could not resist the temptation to pick up the portrait and examine it more closely.

"What a pretty girl," he thought: "brown eyes, decidedly—and black hair:—an Italian, perhaps? Or no, more likely a Russian, with that heart-shaped face, arched eyebrows, and audacious though sensitive mouth."

And here, Leo noticed something which made him open his own mouth, and stare like one bewitched. In the lower corner of the picture was written:

Sonia Bernin,
THE COPPER HOUSE

CHAPTER III

*Wallion Meets B22, and Certain Remarkable Episodes an a
Great Man's Career Are Described, with the Desired Effect*

Maurice Wallion quitted the neighborhood of room 23 rather hurriedly, as
soon as the baron had gone in: not from fear—there was no such word in
his vocabulary—but because, in consequence of this somewhat unexpected
commencement of hostilities, he found himself suddenly involved in a regular network of complicated problems.

Bernard Jenin's unexpected arrival had completely upset his plans, and
forced him to show his hand prematurely to a powerful, prompt and intelligent adversary, who would certainly stick at nothing in the way of frustrat-
ing him. He did not regret the opportunity of dealing the first blow, for his
frankness had probably baffled the baron at the start; but he foresaw that
the approaching struggle would be a fierce though brief one—brief, because in the course of a few hours he must either be definitely beaten, or in
possession of the information which would make it possible for him to
place the matter in the hands of the police. It was, therefore, important for
him to get quickly and surely to work, before Baron Fayerling had had
time to call up reinforcements.

He slipped out of the hotel, and jumped into a tram, bound for the northern district. He wondered which way Jenin had gone, for it disturbed him a
little that he had been able to do nothing for the unfortunate young fellow,
beyond hurrying him away, with an urgent warning to keep clear of Fayerling's spies, and in case of need to take refuge in the offices of the *Daily
Courier*.

There was undoubtedly something mysterious about Jenin himself, but
Wallion consoled himself with the thought that the young man's fate would
soon be settled in one way or another, and he decided to mention the matter
to Robert Lang. For the time being, he had more important business to at-
tend to. The tram turned into Tegnér Street and he got out. He walked
slowly up the street, stopped opposite one of the ugly, gray, five-storied
houses, and began, quite unostentatiously, to watch the windows on the
first floor.

He had known for the last month, that this was one of Ortiz's headquarters, and he suspected that Ortiz himself had stayed there for some time at the beginning of the year. It was ostensibly a Finnish boarding-house, but it was not advertised as such, and there never seemed to be any rooms to let except to lodgers recommended by the baron or by Tassler. For the time being, the only lodgers were three persons who had recently arrived from Russia, and had some sort of regular work at the Finno-Russian Import and Export Company. Rastakov, too, generally stayed there, whenever he did not happen to be at the Copper House. Wallion took it for granted that the man who was known as B.22, and had shadowed Jenin on his journey to Stockholm, would come here, and he was already considering the advisability of setting Robert Lang to watch the house, when he suddenly saw B.22 himself come out of the door, and go quickly down the street.

The journalist was somewhat taken aback by this unexpected apparition; it was quite obvious that something unusual had happened to the spy, for he kept looking round, and Wallion could see that he appeared very nervous.

The journalist thought for a bit. What had happened? B.22 had evidently gone straight to the boarding-house from the hotel, and had apparently found some trouble awaiting him. Nothing was to be seen at the windows.

Feeling rather puzzled, he began to follow the man, who turned hurriedly down one side street after another, behaving more and more strangely. He stood still now and then, staring anxiously behind him with his large dark eyes, and not taking the slightest notice of the journalist; his hands fidgeted in and out of his coat-pockets, and his lips moved as though he were whispering to himself. Then he darted forward again, through a passage that intersected a corner building, and cut across an adjoining churchyard.

Wallion, who began to grow tired of this extraordinary game, stepped quickly up, and tapped him on the shoulder: "Good morning, my friend," he exclaimed, "why this hurry?"

The man started so violently that he nearly fell; Wallion caught hold of him. "Now then, no nonsense!" he said sternly. "I know everything, and I want to have a talk with you. If you tell me the truth, I may be able to help you."

He threw out this remark by way of a feeler, but the man took it literally; a look of relief appeared on his haggard face, and he said doubtfully: "Are you one of Jenin's friends? I don't know you, what do you want with me? Are you a detective, by any chance?" he added suspiciously.

"No, I am a newspaper reporter," said Wallion, still keeping hold of his arm. "Come along with me."

They went into a small, empty café, and sat down at a table in an inner room. B.22 remained silent and watchful, but Wallion left him no time for consideration.

"I won't ask you your real name, B.22," said he, "but you had better be quite straight with me, or it may be the worse for you. You have a rotten set of friends, my lad, and it is high time you quit working with them. Now tell me, what is going on at the boarding-house?"

"Yes, I will tell you," the fellow burst out excitedly. "I will have no more to do with them, they are going too far. I don't want to lose my life...."

His eyes were bloodshot, and he tugged at his collar as though he felt a halter round his neck already. He flung himself suddenly across the table, and seized the journalist by the sleeve. "Help me," he stammered, "I am afraid of them! Ortiz is coming, and he will ruin us all, if nobody can stop him."

Wallion looked sharply at him. He had already observed him in the hotel, and had formed his conclusions as to the man's character. "Since when have you made up your mind to betray Ortiz?"

B.22 hung his head. "Since yesterday," he replied indistinctly. "When Bernard Jenin told me what Tarraschin's memorandum was about, I was afraid to have anything more to do with it—it is altogether too ghastly...."

He really seemed to be hesitating, and Wallion decided to come to the point quickly, for there was no time to waste in unnecessary preliminaries.

"How much do you know about Ortiz?" he asked.

"I? Nothing. They told me that he was the boss, and that we were paid with his money: and he pays well."

Wallion made a movement of disgust. The payment seemed all that this man cared about.

"Have you ever seen Ortiz?"

"No. Baron Fayerling always gave me my orders, and paid me. They say that Ortiz is a rich and powerful man, and that he will soon be one of the greatest persons in Europe. But I have never seen him, and I know nothing of him."

"Well, I am going to tell you something about him; it is because you know so little that you are so much afraid of him. He is one of the most daring adventurers that ever lived, and anyone who espouses his cause is on the road to ruin."

B.22 shuddered, and Wallion watched him narrowly.

"Did you ever hear of the Emperor of the Amazons?" he asked.

B.22 shook his head in surprise.

"Emperor of the Amazons?" he repeated; "it sounds like a farce."

"It was a farce, too, at any rate the newspapers called it so, and it was played seven years ago. A young Brazilian millionaire who had already made himself conspicuous by his lavish and eccentric propensities, concluded one fine day that he could no longer endure the restrictions of life in a community of law-abiding citizens, and his fertile brain, which was always revolving ambitious schemes, decided to create an absolutely new environment.

"His name was Gabriel Napoleon Ortiz, and he was a reputed descendant of Napoleon the Great; he had already been implicated in a formidable scandal in Paris, where he had attempted to organize a Monarchist rising against the Republic, in the hope of getting himself recognized as Napoleon IV. At that time he was only a youth of nineteen, and it was an easy matter to deport him to Brazil. But the lion's claws were not drawn, and by degrees he gathered round him quite a number of adventurers, who aided and abetted him in his far-reaching plans. One day, early in 1910, he steamed away up the River Amazon in his armored pleasure yacht, and disappeared into the interior of Brazil. It was given out that he was subsidizing an expedition for scientific research, but about six months later, the Brazilian Government was astounded to receive a highly-imposing document, signed Gabriel Napoleon I, Emperor of the Amazons, in which the new monarch stated that he had proclaimed himself Emperor over the tracts of land at the sources of the River Amazon, the country being rich and extensive, but chiefly inhabited by Indians. He demanded, first, official recognition by the Brazilian Government, secondly, free access to the River Amazon, and thirdly, an immediate and definite revision of boundary questions. At the same time, through the medium of the South and North American newspapers, he invited enterprising and energetic people to settle as colonists in his dominion, declared his intention of founding a capital, and purchased six liners for passenger traffic down the great river. Of course, the whole thing was impossible; nobody took the man seriously, and the papers treated the matter as a huge joke; it was altogether too farfetched! Before many months had gone by, the Emperor of the Amazons was taken into custody by Brazilian troops: he was found at the head of an army of a hundred and twenty men, which immediately took to flight. He was handed over to his relations, amongst whom was the famous aëroplane-constructor Ortiz; feeling rather crestfallen, he was obliged to consent to leave the country quietly, and nobody gave another thought to the Empire of the Amazons."

"Emperor of the Amazons," muttered B.22 with a laugh. "I do seem to have a hazy recollection of it now. And so that man was Ortiz! I begin to understand...."

The journalist saw that his story had made an impression, and he continued: "You will notice that this Brazilian millionaire-adventurer was not without certain elements of greatness. Such causes as his have prospered before now. It was only that he lived in an age when, under normal circumstances, adventures of that kind are absurd. Public opinion is formed by the Press, and the Press laughed the Empire of the Amazons to scorn. Fifteen years earlier, the man might have succeeded, but, as it was, he had learnt a dearly-bought lesson—till next time! He had not abandoned a single detail of his great project, but he could bide his time: he could go on with his preparations. The next act in the drama was played in New York. Ortiz proved himself a financial genius of the first order, floated one gigantic speculation after another, with truly Napoleonic strategy, and was acclaimed before long as one of Wall Street's brightest stars, or, more correctly, meteors. Finally, he 'swung' a 'corner' in coffee with unscrupulous skill, increased his already colossal fortune tenfold, and gained the nickname of 'The Coffee King.' The Emperor of the Amazons had become a Coffee King! At any rate, you can see what he was aiming at. As 'emperor' he had brought imprisonment on at most forty persons; as 'king' he had ruined thousands. His power for evil had increased, but it was not yet fully developed, and the great opportunity was still to come. He does not advance step by step, like other men. No, his ambition demands constant movement, culminating in some tremendous display of strength. His motto is: 'Better a grand catastrophe than a meagre victory.' Laws do not exist for a man with such ideas, and what can those persons expect who are bold enough to follow him as assistants or subordinates, but a prison cell, or something even worse, for their pains?"

B.22 was listening as though he had been hypnotized, and Wallion went on: "After his 'coup' on the coffee market, Gabriel Ortiz disappeared from New York. He realized his assets and was seen no more in Wall Street. He had attained his primary aim, and provided himself with the means of carrying out even the wildest and most ambitious of his dreams. The episode in the Amazons had taught him experience: in New York he had acquired millions. He was now fully equipped, and only waited for a favorable opportunity. In August, 1914, the Great War broke out."

The journalist sat silent and thoughtful for a little while. Then he continued: "It is horrible to think that a Brazilian freebooter should find the great chance of his lifetime in the grimmest tragedy that has ever befallen the human race. It is true that in this war, as never before, there have been openings for adventurers who are ready to sell their swords or their skill to the highest bidder.

"Within the war-area, where, as in an earthquake, all the powers of darkness rise to the surface, Ortiz found the desired field of operations, where he might sow his millions, and reap an abundant harvest of power. After due calculation, he fixed upon Russia as his objective, and Stockholm as his starting-point. How long have you been in his service?"

"Since October, 1915."

"Nearly from the beginning, then. I can tell by your accent that you are a Finn. I suppose they made you believe that you would be working for the liberty of Finland?"

"That was so," said B.22 in a low voice.

"Do you still think so, now that Finland is really free, in consequence of the March Revolution? Was that Ortiz' work?"

The man crimsoned with rage and shame. He struck his hand on the table, and said: "No, since I got to know the contents of the Tarraschin document, I can see that Ortiz is neither working for freedom nor for the Tsar: he thinks only of himself."

"Exactly," said Wallion, coldly, "and you should have realized that long ago."

"How could I?" replied B.22 piteously; "I knew nothing of him, until you told me all this. What shall I do?"

"Don't take it so hard. You have been too easily tempted by the thought of quickly earned money, that's all, and now you're in a fix. You haven't told me yet what happened in the boarding-house."

"I had only just got there," said B.22 excitedly, "when I heard the telephone ring. One of the Russians answered it, and I was in the room alongside. I guessed that Rastakov had rung up, and I heard the Russian say: 'Yes, he has just come in.' They were speaking about me, and I was alarmed to hear the man say: 'We had better shadow him; it would be easier to get rid of him in Finland than here. Yes, we will keep an eye on him; if he gives any trouble, we will find a way which won't attract attention. No, he hasn't spoken to anyone yet....' Then I was sure that my fate was sealed, and at first I felt paralyzed with fear, but I knew that they would be after me in a few seconds, and, without even stopping to get my knapsack, I crept downstairs, and out of the house...."

Wallion could not help pitying the poor fellow, who looked like a man sentenced to death, and could hardly speak coherently.

"Was that all?" he asked.

"It was quite enough for me; they mean to do something dreadful.... I am not the first...."

"I know. I will help you on one condition: has our conversation convinced you how necessary it is for you to tell me honestly and openly everything that may lead to the annihilation of Ortiz and his gang?"

"Yes, yes, only tell me what I can do."

"You won't only think of saving your own skin? You promise to help me to the best of your ability?"

"Yes, yes, that's just what I want to do; only save me!"

The man's sincerity was undoubted; Wallion's earnestness had entirely conquered his feeble will. He gazed at the journalist with doglike submission, whilst the latter wrote a few lines, and his address, on a card.

"Take this," he said, "go straight to my house in the Valhalla Road, and hand the card to my housekeeper. Stay there till I come. Just wait a minute, while I telephone to her."

B.22 seized the card with an audible sigh of relief and gratitude. The journalist went into the outer room, and rang up his house. The housekeeper answered, and he informed her briefly what she was to do with B.22, and what further precautions he must observe. Then, after a little consideration, he rang up the offices of the *Daily Courier*, and asked for Robert Lang, who came at once to the telephone. "Has anyone been to ask for me?" said Wallion. "What? Leonard Grath? He's just gone? What a nuisance, I wanted particularly to see him. Don't you know where he has gone? He really is far too headstrong to be allowed to go off by himself, you should have kept him. No, I can't come up at present, I must go and see what the baron and Tassler are up to, but I want you to come at once to Tegnér Street, and find out what is going on at the boarding-house there, if you can. It is probable that we shall soon have to give official information to the police; we ought to have sufficient proof in our hands in a few hours' time. Look here: before you leave the office, arrange for somebody trustworthy—say, Steno Beyler—to receive a young man named Bernard Jenin, who may turn up there in the course of the day, and not to let him out of his sight before I have had a word with him. Yes, that's all, I can tell you more later; I've a big job on hand at present...."

He put down the receiver, and returned to the other room, but he stopped short on the threshold: B.22 had disappeared. A door leading to the passage stood open, and on the table lay a paper, with a few hurried lines scrawled upon it. Wallion snatched it up, and ran into the passage. After glancing into the garden, which was surrounded by a high wall, he went out into the street, but B.22 was nowhere to be seen. Feeling very anxious, the journalist read what was written on the paper: "I must go. One of them is outside in the churchyard, and I am sure he has seen me at the window. If they get to know that I have anything to do with you, they will shoot me in the street. Expect me early—about seven—tomorrow morning."

The journalist crumpled up the paper and put it in his pocket, after which he lighted a cigarette. Not a single person was visible in the whole length of the silent street.

CHAPTER IV

Leonard Grath Acts on His Own Responsibility and Meets with a Girl Who Runs Away from Him

Leo left the problem-hunter's room like a man in a dream. It did not occur to him to wait for Robert Lang's return, but when he got out into the street, he found himself still holding the photograph in his hand. Ought he not to put it back on Wallion's table? He looked hesitatingly at it: "Sonia Bernin, the Copper House," he read once more. "So that's Andrei Bernin's daughter. Well, there hasn't been such a beautiful girl in the Copper House these last fifty years!" There spoke the artist; an ordinary man would perhaps have called the girl striking, but certainly not beautiful. Her face was not oval, but rather of an aquiline type; her mouth was no Cupid's bow, but boyishly firm, above a self-willed chin. But the large, dark eyes beneath their black, wing-like brows, had a mysterious attraction for him—it seemed as though they were calling to him, and the artist in him listened—who knows, perhaps the man also!

Burchardt's story, Wallion's warnings, vanished in a moment from Leo's mind. He put the photograph into his pocket and made his way to the general station, where he went up to the booking-office, and demanded: "A single to Karkby." A philosopher could no doubt draw many ingenious deductions from this simple action, knowing that it was to influence his future to an extraordinary degree. But Leo, who was anything but a philosopher, did not give the matter a thought, and, having received a scrap of brown pasteboard in exchange for a few silver coins, he made his way past all obstructions to the platform, where the train for Nynäs stood blowing off steam. He studied with a critical eye the effect of the sun shining through the puffs of steam, and made a mental note of the colors, "Pink and silver in the sunlight, violet in the shade." With that, he got into the train. He had chosen the last compartment, which was still quite empty, but a minute later, one other passenger entered, and sat quietly down opposite. He was a young or middle-aged man, in a threadbare overcoat: his tired face was pale, almost grayish, the eyes encircled with innumerable tiny wrinkles; the neat leathern attaché-case which he carried in his hand seemed to cause him some anxiety, for he evidently debated with himself whether he should put it up in the rack, then cast an uneasy glance at Leo, and finally decided to keep it on his knee. Leo's amused expression appeared to embarrass the man, for he stared straight in front of him, with that air of constraint which betrays that one feels oneself under observation. At the same time, he seemed to be listening for something outside, and Leo heard him give a little sigh of relief when the train gave a sudden jerk, and steamed out of the station, with rapidly-increasing speed. They were alone in the carriage, that is, in their half of it, for it was divided into two sections, with a gangway between. Leo's thoughts began to wander. He felt curious and rather excited at the thought of what he should find when he arrived at the Copper House. The recollection that he would soon have no right to go there made him serious again. Take it all in all, he had certainly been a thoughtless, easy-going fellow! In a flash of clear-sighted self-criticism, he passed the last few years in review: gay parties at the studio in Montmartre, seaside amusements at Ostend, yachting, tennis and garden-parties in California—one long, sunny playtime in company with other idlers, who talked a great deal, and accomplished little. And now, what was the result? He must sell the Copper House, and tune his life to a new key, with less play and more work…it was jolly hard lines!

The conductor came round to clip the tickets, and as Leo put his back into his pocket, his fingers came in contact with the photograph, and he took it out for another look. Presently he heard a movement, and the sound of a deep breath quite close to him, and he looked up. His fellow-passenger had bent forward and was gazing at the photograph with wide-open eyes, but in a second he drew back, like a snail into its shell, without meeting Leo's inquiring glance. The man sat perfectly motionless, with his hands on his case, staring at the opposite wall as before, but his lips were twitching, and his face, as Leo put it to himself, had no more color in it than a pencil drawing. All of a sudden Leo remembered Wallion's warning, the disappearance of his pocket-book, the man with the camera, and Burchardt's anxious face. He felt convinced that the strange figure opposite had been desperately startled by the sight of the photograph, and he began to feel a chill suspicion that he was somehow or other getting entangled in a huge net, which was gradually tightening its meshes round him. What was up? Was everybody going crazy?

He resolved to say something, but changed his mind as hastily, for the other man looked as impassive as an image of Buddha. The situation was becoming awkward, and meanwhile the train rattled on towards Nynäs and the sea. Leo quitted the field, and took refuge at the nearest passage-window. Refreshed by the strong sea-breeze, he made a laudable attempt to sum up the experiences of this eventful day, but soon tired of this, and began instead to gaze aimlessly at the passing landscape. Could he have guessed that the most eventful part of the day was still to come, he would perhaps have jumped out of the train then and there, and returned to Stockholm; but, not being endowed with second-sight, he alighted calmly at Karkby station. The first person he saw as he reached the platform was the stranger with the attaché-case, who left the train at the same time by another door. Leo saw him go up to the pointsman and address him in good Swedish. Seeing a look of surprise pass over the pointsman's face, the young man could not repress his curiosity but strolled past them, and heard the pointsman exclaim: "Well, if it's to the Copper House you are going, I doubt if you'll find yourself very welcome."

"You think not?" said the man, in a low, nervous voice; "may I venture to ask why?"

"We never hear of there being any entertaining out there nowadays: a nice sort of life they must lead. If it was a monastery they couldn't shut themselves up more," added the pointsman mysteriously, as he watched the train disappear round a curve.

"A pack of foreigners, too; I suppose it's this here wretched war which brings them over. Sweden's full of these heathen now, and they have to have bread-tickets.... Well, if you must go to the Copper House, it will take you the best part of half an hour to walk it...."

Leo walked on out of earshot, and did not feel inclined to pass them again, as he wished to avoid recognition. He crossed the railway, and walked slowly past some newly-built villas, and the old deaf florist's green-house ("wonder if the old boy is still alive?"). As he reached the outskirts of the wood, he turned round and saw the man with the case walking about a hundred yards behind him, like a gray shadow on the white road. The fellow, like himself, was really on the way to the Copper House, then? He looked down at the dark, solitary figure, approaching in the sunshine, and wondered what he had better do: leave things as they were, or force a closer acquaintance. But he was not called upon to make a decision after all, for the other left the road suddenly, leapt over a ditch, and vanished into the woods.

* * * *

A quarter of an hour later, Leo stood outside the so-called Karka gates. And here we must insert a bit of topography which will help our readers to a clearer understanding of the events which followed.

The port and watering-place of Nynäs is, so to speak, Stockholm's most southerly outpost on the Baltic Sea, as Saltsjöbaden and Sandhamn are its most easterly ones. The Nynäs railway runs throughout the length of Söderström which lies between those two points, and the nearer it gets to

Nynäs, the narrower grows the hilly country between the railway and the sea. As Karkby is one of the last stations before Nynäs, one can easily reach the shore by walking for about half an hour in an easterly direction. But, as the railway is a fairly recent innovation, anyone who starts to walk, soon strikes the old main-road to Stockholm (nowadays practically disused), and, by following it, he will come suddenly upon the entrance to Karka, rising, as if by magic, out of the deserted landscape. It is a ruinous archway, with rusty iron gates, and a porter's lodge, behind which a carriage-road winds up through an avenue of ancient trees. No house is visible, but this is the boundary of the Graths' ancestral property, Karka, which occupies a considerable portion of land between the sea and the road. It is strangely impressive to see, in the midst of the wooded country, this once stately entrance left desolate and crumbling, like a monument to the wealth and prosperity of former times.

What was the state of affairs at the Copper House, as the whole property was generally called, from the appearance of the house itself, we shall tell in due time.

Leonard Grath, its present owner (and that only in name), stood outside the gates, and looked through the bars. Outside the porter's lodge sat a man cleaning a double-barreled gun; he did not look up.

"Hullo, there!" cried the young man cheerily, "just let me in, there's a good chap."

The fellow looked into the road with evident surprise; he had a swarthy, sunburnt face.

"Who are you and what do you want?" he demanded roughly, and without getting up.

"I am Leonard Grath, the owner of the Copper House, and I want to come in."

The man stared at Leo with an insolent grin, and said: "Indeed, you want to come in, do you? Why not say at once that you are the Emperor of China?"

"Don't you hear me say that this place belongs to me? Open the gate at once, man!" exclaimed Leo angrily, and shaking the locked gate violently. The porter slipped a cartridge into his gun, and laid the weapon across his knees.

"Don't you go trying that on," said he. "If you are the owner, you are in California, and I guess you won't mind if I send a charge of shot in your direction...."

He cocked his gun and raised it.

"Be off, now," he added, "we are tired of sending strangers off the place."

Leo returned his look, and retired unwillingly, but he could not help laughing: the situation struck him as supremely ridiculous.

"You may see my papers," said he.

"Don't talk to me of your papers!" replied the man, following up his words with a most unexpected action. Raising the gun, and without getting up, he fired. The range was too short for the shot to spread, but Leo saw chips of mortar fly from the gateway.

"You—you scoundrel!" he burst out in amazement. "What do you mean by that?"

The man loaded again, without a word. They looked at one another; Leo opened his mouth, closed it again, and returned to the road: he was not inclined to laugh any longer. He walked cautiously alongside the iron palings, for he knew that they came to an end about a hundred yards further on, where a rustic fence took their place. When he was out of sight from the gate, he clambered over the fence, and found himself at length on his own property, with every inch of which he had been familiar since childhood. He made his way up a slope, and came to a small pine wood, which, after a little consideration, he entered by a well-worn path. Suddenly he stopped, and drew a deep breath. "Home!" he said aloud. The thought filled him with ecstasy; he had not expected that the sight of this old-world, sun-steeped spot would move him so deeply, and he sat down on a stone to recover himself. To think that he was really home again, and that, in another ten minutes, he would be inside the Copper House! Forgetting everything else, he sprang up, and set off with swift, eager steps in the direction of a field which could be seen through the trees.

At that minute he heard a light footstep on the path ahead of him, and a girl in a black riding-habit came running towards him, looking behind her at every few steps. Two men with guns slung at their backs could be seen some way off on the left, hastening with long strides, as though to intercept her. The girl uttered a cry, as the two men leapt down on the path just in front of her, and seized her by the arms. She easily shook them off, and her riding-whip left a red wheal on the face of the nearest. They said something in a rough voice, and the girl cried out angrily: "I shall go where I like, you have no right...."

"You be quiet, now, Miss, and go home to your Papa," said one of the men, not uncivilly; and he lifted her up, and began to carry her back along the same path by which they had come. She broke loose, and struck him again across the face. The pain made him furious, and with a shout, he pushed her violently away. By this time Leo had come up. "We don't treat women like that, in this part of the world," said he, pushing the fellow aside with a shove of his broad shoulder. The second man reached for his gun, but Leo twisted the weapon out of his hands, and motioned him back. "Keep still!" he ordered.

The girl had recovered herself, and looked at him in silence. She appeared to be about seventeen or eighteen, and the young man immediately recognized the dark beauty of the photograph. He raised his hat.

"Miss Bernin, I believe? My name is Leonard Grath."

As the girl stood looking uneasily at him, with a curious blank expression in her big brown eyes, he added hastily: "Are you hurt?"

She came up to him, laid both hands on his arm, and said in a low tone: "Go! Go back the way you came!"

Leo glanced at the two men, who stood a little way off between him and the path, watching him attentively.

"What are those two fellows doing?" he asked.

"They are two of the forest-guards," answered the girl, "but do, do go away!"

"Why should I?" said Leo, with a pang of annoyance and disappointment. "I have a right to come here, haven't I?"

He offered her his arm, rather ironically, and added: "Although I seem to be so unwelcome, allow me to escort you to the Copper House; I am just on my way there."

The girl colored, bit her lip, and, turning round, she walked away. One of the men laughed, and Leo said sharply, glad of the opportunity to give vent to the wrath that was boiling within: "Be quiet, if you don't want me to thrash you off the premises! I have evidently arrived unexpectedly, but I haven't begun yet. Just wait a bit, and you'll see!"

The two men gave no sign that they had heard what he had said. Leo threw down the gun, turned his back, and followed the girl. When he caught her up, she hung her head, and he saw that she was very pale. He fell into step at her left side, but she walked on as though she was alone.

"There seem to be great changes here," he remarked, without taking any notice of her attitude. "The Copper House was always famous for its hospitality, but now it seems that it won't even admit its own master."

He paused, but there was no reply.

"As for forest-guards," he continued, "such luxuries have been superfluous in these woods for many years past. I suppose you keep them to look after the squirrels? At any rate, one of them evidently took me for a squirrel...."

He described, with a sort of bitter enjoyment, the episode at the gate. Quite unexpectedly the girl burst into tears and he looked at her with sudden remorse.

"I am a brute," he muttered. "Miss Bernin, for Heaven's sake, look at me, you can see and hear that I'm only an awful idiot. Please do laugh at me instead!"

There was a sort of tearful laugh, then a sob, and finally the laugh won the day. The girl looked up at him, and dried her eyes with a little silk handkerchief.

"It is silly to cry," she remarked seriously. "Were you very surprised?"

"Not so very," he assured her. "Young ladies are allowed to shed a few tears now and then, aren't they? It is perfectly natural…."

"I have forgotten to thank you," she said, with a little bow. "It wasn't as dangerous as it looked, but you came up at the right moment. You see, my father and my aunt are very strict, and occasionally I rebel, and the authorities send out the squirrel-police to quell the disturbance. You arrived on the final scene of a domestic crisis…."

The little lady was chattering away in the liveliest fashion with quick, bird-like movements of her uncovered, dark head, which made the jet earrings that she wore dance and quiver. She stepped out like a boy, with a quick, firm tread, swinging her riding-whip.

"You say now that I came at the right minute," said Leo reproachfully, "but just before that you told me to go away!"

"Don't you mean to?" she asked, with a rapid glance from a pair of eyes that just then struck him as being as dark as night.

"Not unless you ask me to again," he replied boldly.

The girl stopped and turned round. "Things haven't altered, you know," she said, and walked on. Leo looked round also. The two forest-guards were still standing amongst the trees, looking down at them, but a third had joined them, and each of the three men held his gun in his hands.

The young man felt a little shiver pass through him. Ahead of him, though still some way off, he could see the greater part of the old avenue, which stretched for more than a mile from Karka gates to the house itself, which was still hidden behind some rising ground to the left. He thought he caught sight of two or three figures patrolling the avenue under the shade of the trees, but they vanished before he was quite certain. He began to wonder whether the girl by his side had given him the full explanation of the scene in the wood, but his thoughts took another turn, for now, through the thick foliage, he had a glimpse of the ponderous gables of the house, looking as though they were moulded in green copper. The house, at all events, had not changed in appearance. He stopped on the terrace with its crumbling balustrade, and his eyes drank in the familiar scene, till the dust of years was blown away, and he was a boy once more. There was the square, massive building, its walls weather-stained and gray with age, supporting the steep copper-sheathed roof, which, from its peculiar slope, seemed half as high as the house, and looked like a mediæval helmet, profaned by two tiers of windows; there were the two copper statues of Fortune with her cornucopia, and Mercury with his winged heels, a forgotten figure on either side of the steps, gazing blankly and silently at one another from their never-changing positions.

CHAPTER V

In Which It Is Obvious That
the Owner Is a Guest in His Own House

Leonard Grath entered the Copper House like a visitor, hat in hand. A sunbeam lay right across the polished oak floor of the hall, and in the middle of the patch of light stood a tall, old lady, as upright as a grenadier, and as thin and dark as a Bedouin, who fixed a penetrating glance upon the newcomer. She went on crocheting a piece of lace, the other end of which was hidden in an old-fashioned basket-work satchel that hung on her left arm.

Leo stopped short, as though her look was an actual barrier, and bowed.

"Sonia Andreievna," said the old lady, in the tone of a drill sergeant on parade, "where have you been?"

The girl shot a covert glance at the young man, and threw down her riding-whip.

"Aunt Lona," she replied meekly, "this gentleman has just been mistaken for a squirrel…."

"Sonia Andreievna," the sharp voice interrupted, "speak sensibly; you know that I detest riddles."

"My name is Leonard Grath," the latter interposed, hastily, bowing again and feeling somewhat embarrassed.

The crochet-needles came to a standstill, and their owner took two strides towards him, and stared unblinkingly into his eyes. He noticed that, in spite of her iron-gray hair and lean, dried-up looks, she could hardly be more than sixty. Her imperious eyes still flashed with youthful energy, every movement betokened strength, and her whole bearing was that of a well-bred lady, even though she might be a bit of a martinet. Like her niece, she was plainly dressed in black, with white ruffles, and a necklace of jet beads, which clicked gently as she moved.

"Leonard Grath," she echoed; "the owner?"

"Yes, I am afraid I have arrived rather unexpectedly, and if I have in any way…."

"Sonia Andreievna! Pick up your whip at once" (the young man was quite startled) "and put it in its place. Yes, Mr. Grath, I cannot deny that you *have* taken us by surprise."

"Oh dear, I certainly never meant…."

"Sonia Andreievna! Do you see what time it is? Have I not told you a thousand times that we have a fixed hour for dinner?"

Her remarks seemed to Leo to be emphasized by a perfect regiment of exclamation-points, and he did not wonder that the girl darted away like an arrow from a bow. But to his surprise, no sooner were they alone, than the old lady's tone became almost cordial.

"I am Lona Ivanovna Bernin, and as your tenant I bid you welcome to the Copper House. You will give us the pleasure of your company at dinner? Good, let us have a cigarette while we are waiting."

Still wondering, Leo allowed himself to be ushered to an armchair in the familiar old Empire drawing-room on the left side of the hall. Lona Ivanovna offered him a cigarette case, and herself took a Russian cigarette, which she lighted with one hand. Leo was thinking what to say next, when she forestalled him.

"Have you come from abroad?"

"Yes, from California."

"Ah, California; a magnificent climate, I believe. No doubt you have become tired of living out there?"

"Not exactly, but I felt inclined to come home."

"Hm—Do you think of making a long stay?"

"That depends. You see, it isn't a question of climate, exactly…."

She pursed up her mouth and frowned.

"In my opinion, the climate of California is far preferable," she remarked, looking sharply at him.

"Very possibly, but this visit will be quite a change for me."

"How so?"

"Oh, there is so much that is new, I mean…a whole lot of strange… well, in short…."

Leo stopped short in confusion, and puffed away furiously at his cigarette. The old lady blew a perfect ring, looked quizzically at him through it, and said dryly: "Young man, whatever you do, don't go and fall in love with Sonia!"

Leo stared dumbfounded at his cigarette. The conversation dropped, and silence reigned in the room, broken only by the buzzing of a stray bee on the window pane.

* * * *

Dinner was over, and Leonard Grath the richer by several experiences. First of all, he had proved the truth of the old adage that: "guests are hosts in the host's house," for was not he a guest and stranger, and moreover a thoroughly unwelcome one, in his own home? It seemed to him as though the girl and her aunt took it in turns to keep an eye on him: he could see them exchanging glances and whispers whose meaning was unintelligible to him, and, what struck him as strangest of all, in the whole of that spacious house and its adjoining buildings there appeared to be no living creature except the two ladies. He inquired, as a matter of politeness, for Mr. Andrei Bernin, who was stated to be in bed in his own room, and far too unwell to see the honored guest.

As soon as the dinner was over, Sonia, obeying a signal from her aunt, proposed a turn round the garden, and the two young people strolled along for a while in silence. It was getting towards sunset, and the rural orchestra was in full chorus: birds were fluting in a medley of youthful emulation, bumble-bees droned in their drowsy baritones, and in the grass the crickets added their violin notes to the evening concert.

Now that Sonia Bernin in the flesh was alongside of him, Leo found her ten times more interesting than when he had first seen her portrait on Wallion's table; her boyish unconstraint, added to a lissom, almost kitten-like grace, and her ready wit, gave him a delightful sensation of comradeship—but the minute he attempted to strike a note of intimacy, he ran up against a barrier of chilly reserve, and the pose of the boyish, black head became all of a sudden alarmingly ladylike. Whatever the reason might be, she appeared totally unimpressed by his masculine superiority, and this was a very novel experience for the spoilt young man.

At length he remarked: "I had thought of staying some time at the Copper House, but it seems to me I am rather 'de trop' here."

She twisted a leaf between her lips like a cigarette: "How so?" she inquired.

"Oh, there's no doubt about it. The man at the gate showed it quite unmistakably—for one."

"With his gun, you mean? It *was* too bad; but you see, he naturally took you for an impostor, having heard that the owner of the Copper House was in America. I expect he will be discharged, in any case," she added.

"And you told me yourself to go away, as soon as ever you knew who I was," he continued.

"Wasn't it kind of me to warn you, when it is so dull here?" laughed the girl.

"It is not dull here, and that is not why you warned me," he retorted. She looked up, and their eyes met: for the second time that day, Leo saw hers dilate and darken. She did not reply, but hurried on a little, as though to evade him, but he kept step with her, and proceeded:

"As you know, your father wants to buy this property; it is a pity I can't have a talk with him about it. Your aunt is reticent, and you are mysterious.

Won't you have a little pity on me?"

They had walked to the top of a slight rise, from which they could see down the greater part of the avenue. The girl stood still, panting a little. Suddenly she asked:

"Have you seen Mr. Tassler?"

Leo shook his head, and they were silent again. The girl seemed to be listening to something, rather uneasily. Far off in the sunlit stillness a rhythmical throbbing sound became audible; it approached with uncanny rapidity, getting louder every minute, then suddenly ceased altogether.

"Did you hear that?" whispered the girl.

"Yes," he answered. "A motor cycle has apparently stopped at Karka gates; it's a pity we can't see them from here, it must be someone from Stockholm."

As he said this, he remembered the young man with the attaché-case, whom he had so unintentionally startled with Sonia's photograph, but as he was about to tell her of the occurrence, there was a dramatic interruption. A shot was fired at the gate, and it was followed by a long, thrilling cry. A few seconds later, a man came dashing up the avenue as though he was running for his life. Leo at once recognized his fellow passenger, and the girl cried out in a voice of terrified dismay: "Sergius, Sergius!"

The fugitive raised his face, which was deathly pale, and without stopping, he exclaimed: "Rastakov!"

The girl turned round to Leo, and said in a rapid stifled voice: "Hide yourself; and, mind, you have seen nothing!"

With that, she sprang down from the little hill, followed by the fugitive, and both disappeared. Almost immediately afterwards, two more men came running up the avenue: one was the porter who had threatened Leo with the same gun that he still carried in his hand, the other was a tall fellow, dressed as a motor cyclist. They also vanished in the direction of the house.

Without further delay, Leo hastened back along the same path by which he had come, and in five seconds he came in sight of the terrace in front of the Copper House. He saw the man with the case run up the steps, hesitate for a moment, then dash into the house. The girl followed on his heels, and the porter and the cyclist reached the terrace to find it deserted. Then, as though by the touch of a magic wand, some more men appeared from both sides of the house. These, with the two men already mentioned, made a party of nine, of whom four carried guns. They approached the house at the double. The cyclist called out some order in a commanding voice, and began to mount the terrace-steps. Leo reached the spot at the same moment, and exclaimed: "What's wrong?"

The motor cyclist took no notice of him.

Again a shot rang out, this time inside the Copper House; most of the men had passed out of earshot on the other side of the house, but the cyclist, the porter, and one other unknown man, ran into the hall, together with Leo.

The old lady advanced to meet them, with a revolver in her hand. She looked firmly and menacingly at the intruder and said: "Rastakov, did I invite you to come in?"

The cyclist halted.

"Who fired, Lona Ivanovna?" he demanded.

"I did."

"Where is he?"

"Whom do you mean?"

"Oh, you know perfectly well, that thief Bernard Jenin; what have you done with him?"

Lona Ivanovna thrust the revolver into her workbag, looked resignedly at the cyclist, and said: "You may look for him."

Leo, who understood nothing of this hurried interchange of questions, looked on bewildered. Rastakov caught sight of the fugitive's case lying open on the floor, caught it up, and flung it against the wall with an oath, for it was empty.

"I will have him, dead or alive," he shouted, "and the damned document too!"

He ran half-way up the stairs to the first floor, but turned round as though he had remembered something.

"And what's more," he cried across the hall, "I know how pigheaded you are, Lona Ivanovna! All right, if you would rather have the Chief to deal with, just let me know! But beware of meddling with Tarraschin's memorandum, for it means death!"

With that, he disappeared. Lona Ivanovna took Leo by the arm, and drew him with unexpected force, though not unkindly, into the dining-room after her.

"Isn't it a case for the police?" he began.

"Don't mix yourself up in this," she said kindly. "Sonia, they want to search the house: you must see that Mr. Grath is spared hearing anything more of Rastakov,…."

Sonia came up to them; she was very pale, but quite composed; the boyish look had vanished, and she answered quietly: "If Mr. Grath is determined to stay, I am afraid he will be obliged to see a good deal both of Rastakov and of Baron Fayerling."

The two women looked expectantly at him. They could hear the hasty steps of the searchers echoing through the whole house.

"I should like to know who this Rastakov is, that he takes so much upon himself in a house where my honored guests are staying," said Leo, emphasizing the word 'guests'—"neither have I heard anything of Baron Fayerling. But I shall be glad to make the acquaintance of anyone who is good enough to honor the Copper House with his presence."

He was quite aware that his tone was not courteous, in spite of the formality of his speech, but he was thoroughly roused. He could see now, as though a curtain had been drawn back, that these people, whose strange dark faces were stamped with furtive menace, were the mysterious offspring of the lurid shadows of the World War.

He thought of the panic-stricken fugitive whom he had just seen flying for his life; of the shot which had so recently rung through the house: of Lona Ivanovna with the revolver in her hand. The frenzied search was still progressing overhead; footsteps and voices echoed through the passages. "Living or dead!" As Rastakov's words recurred to Leo's mind, he was seized with the horrible conviction that murder had been committed already: what ought he to do?

The two women were watching his face as though they longed to read his thoughts.

"Your room is quite ready," said the elder one gravely.

Before Leo had decided what to answer, he found himself alone. He began to pace up and down in great perturbation. He could see one of the men, with his gun, outside on the terrace, silhouetted against the rosy, sunset sky. For the last few minutes, such a silence had fallen, that he could have fancied himself alone in the house. He listened attentively, but could hear nothing. His thoughts circled irresolutely over what had occurred, but he could find no explanation of it, and began to feel more and more uneasy. An hour passed by, the shadows lengthened and still no sound broke the stillness. Was no one coming back?

At last he could bear the suspense no longer, and he went into the hall. He could still see, through the glass doors, the armed sentry on the terrace, but inside the house all was empty and silent. He went from one room to another, and ran upstairs to the first floor, but not a soul did he meet. The thought that the fugitive was perhaps lying dead, huddled away in some dark corner, obsessed him like a nightmare, and his limbs trembled as though with fever. Suddenly a sort of panic came over him, he ran breathlessly up another flight of stairs, burst open the door of his bedroom, and shut it after him with a bang that resounded through the house. Leaning against the door, and alone in the little room, where everything was just as it always had been since his earliest childhood, and where he had dreamed so many boyish dreams, he breathed again.

"Have I gone mad?" he asked himself. "What is going on here? The Problem-hunter was right, the Copper House is full of mysteries!"

He looked round for some water, for his lips felt parched, but there was none in the room. "Can they have killed him!" he thought. "And is it possible that I have stood by, without moving a finger, and allowed a man to be done to death!"

At last he heard a door creak outside, and he peeped out into the dusky corridor. The door of the spare bedroom at the other end of the passage was opening slowly, an inch at a time, and he could see first a feeble, bony hand, and then a stooping figure outlined against the window behind.

The figure moved uncertainly, groping with a stick along the edge of the carpet, and walked with short, senile steps towards the stairs. Leo watched him narrowly, trying to get a glimpse of his face; he thought he could make out a short white beard and straggling white hair under a velvet skull-cap, and the glimmer of a pair of blue spectacles. A blind man! In an instant he realized that his wealthy tenant, Andrei Bernin, was before him for the first time. The old man seemed to hesitate, and called softly: "Sonia!" but receiving no answer, he finally went towards the staircase, tapping with his stick at every step. Leo could hear his quavering voice calling to Lona Ivanovna, the sound getting fainter as it receded. There was something so eerie about those feeble tones, uttered in the silent, lonely house at nightfall, that the young man, with a shudder, shut himself into his room again. After a minute he double-locked the door, and went over to the open window. The sky had faded to sulphur-yellow in the west, and night was closing in, cool and dim, over the countryside. A soft breeze was blowing in from the sea. He heard the crunching of gravel under his window, and leaned out. Two figures passed beneath, one of whom pointed upwards, and said something in an imperious tone. Leo fancied he recognized Rastakov's voice.

They knew, then, that he was in his bedroom, and they were keeping an eye on him! The conviction awakened fresh misgivings. He sat down on the bed, and buried his head in his hands. Was he afraid? Yes, he had to confess that he *was* afraid, because there was nobody within reach in whom he could confide, or whom he could ask for advice…. The Problem-hunter! He sprang to his feet.

Five minutes later, he had climbed down the thick clumsy copper gutter-spout, with the same soundless agility, and the same intense excitement as had characterized such escapades twenty years ago. He expected to be halted by a challenge from the shadowy avenue, but none came, and the owner of Copper House crept away like a Red Indian through the trees into the wood. Three times he caught a glimpse of the dark forms of the men whom Sonia Bernin called forest-guards, but, lucky for once, he did not attract their notice. When he turned round, he could see in the far distance, behind the top of the massive pile of the Copper House, a flickering, bluish glimmer, which seemed to come from the direction of the Bay. He did not venture to delay that he might investigate the source of this unusual light…. When he strung himself aboard the last train to Stockholm, which was already moving out of Karkby, he was gasping for breath, and drenched with perspiration.

CHAPTER VI

The Problem-Hunter

It was past midnight, when a young man, evidently dead-tired, and looking thoroughly exhausted, entered the office of the night Editor of the *Daily Courier*, and asked to see Maurice Wallion. The night Editor, a somewhat callous personage, looked at him without any special interest.

"Wallion?" he answered dryly. "He's not here."

"Where can I find him?"

"That's more than I can tell you—we haven't seen him ourselves! There is just one chance in a thousand that he's at home, but if he is, he doesn't answer the telephone, anyway—I have tried! He won't be best pleased when he sees how his office here has been turned upside down."

"Upside down?"

"That's putting it mildly. You might tell him, if you find him, that his room looks as though a squad of small hurricanes had been performing war-dances in it, and that nobody knows how or when. Here's his address, if you really feel you want the exercise of a night ramble from here to Valhalla Road."

The Editor pushed a scrap of paper into Leo's hand, and showed him out with a polite, though rather suggestive, zeal.

The young man stood for a while in the deserted street, to collect his thoughts. He also turned up his coat-collar, for the keen air made him shiver after his exertions in the wood; and with a gesture of undaunted resolution, he started on his pilgrimage through the shadowy wilderness of stone, beneath the rows of extinguished street lamps.

Women accosted him with inviting glances and alluring voices: and knots of revelers passed him with discordant bursts of laughter; further on, a policeman with his hands behind him, stood gazing after him.

These shadows, appearing and vanishing in the mists of night, recalled the events of the last few hours, as did the glaring, owl-like orbs of the clock-tower, and he hastened his steps, breaking into an occasional run.

When he at last reached the broad, lonely Valhalla Road, past the Stadion and the barracks, his clothes were clinging to him, and he was quite out of breath. It now occurred to him for the first time, that the outer door of the block of flats, in one of which the Problem-hunter lived, would probably be locked, but when he arrived there, he saw that it was partly open, and, without stopping to consider the reason for this, he ran quickly up the stairs....

He came to a standstill before the folding-doors, which bore a brass plate with the name of Maurice Wallion. One of the doors stood ajar, and on the stone floor of the lobby were scattered several splinters of white wood. He heard the stairs creaking on the next landing, as though someone were making his escape that way, startled by his unexpected arrival. All was dark in front of him, but he pushed the door open and stepped over the threshold.

A hand hovered above his head like a swooping hawk and seized him by the neck. The owner of the hand came out from behind the door, and a strong voice said mockingly in his ear: "Come along in, young fellow! No, don't struggle, I've been waiting for you impatiently. I can't say you are much of a hand at forcing a Yale lock, it has taken you the best part of half an hour—and now—glad to see you, take a seat!"

With what seemed to Leo superhuman strength, he was lifted up and flung headlong into a corner, where he fell on to a heap of something soft, clothes evidently. The electric light was turned on with a click, and he saw bending over him a tall man in shooting costume. A pair of keen gray eyes, that sparkled with energy and humor, were peering down at him, and Leo guessed instinctively who this must be.

"Good morning, Mr. Wallion," he said. "Pleased to meet you...."

"It's you, is it?" answered the Problem-hunter, without seeming in the least taken aback. "Why are you sitting there?"

Leo got up.

"I was under the impression that there was an earthquake just as I came in, but perhaps I was mistaken!"

"It was I who was mistaken, my dear Mr. Grath. One of Baron Fayerling's aides-de-camp has been playing about with the lock of my door for the last half-hour, and I have been standing behind the door waiting—naturally they thought I was out—and just as he was on the point of getting in, you interrupted him, and fell into my trap instead...."

The Problem-hunter broke off, and sprang to the door, but at the same instant, they heard a terrific clattering down the stairs, and the outer door at the bottom was banged to.

"He had evidently no wish to wait, when he knew that I was at home," remarked Wallion. "I must really beg your pardon for the very rough reception I gave you just now. The blackguard, he has quite ruined this lock:

however, that's easily remedied—just a minute, and then we shall be able to have our little chat in comfort."

As he spoke, he was quickly and deftly screwing a strong bolt on the door.

"There, that will do. Now, will you come this way?"

They went into the study, and Wallion lighted a lamp with a yellow shade, that stood upon his writing-table.

"Of course, you are very much surprised at my knowing you again," inquired Wallion, looking with interest, though not disconcertingly so, at his belated visitor, whilst he brought out the ingredients for a refreshing drink of "Johnnie Walker" and soda, fetched cigarettes, and drew the curtains. "You see, I got to know what you looked like as much as three months ago...."

"That didn't surprise me so much," said Leo, who felt quite revived, as he glanced round him at the comfortable room, with its bookshelves and tables. "But how on earth did you know that I was coming to Stockholm? Not two months ago, I hadn't an idea of it myself!"

"A sudden fancy, I suppose?"

"Yes, something put it into my mind, I don't know exactly what...."

"And the minute you get back, you find yourself in a whirlpool of the most extraordinary events?"

"Extraordinary hardly expresses them!"

Maurice Wallion smiled, and sat down opposite Leo.

"I am afraid I owe you another apology," said he. "So you don't exactly know why you came to Stockholm? I can tell you—it was to help me. Yes, I know, you will say that you were not even aware of my existence, until you got my letter in Burchardt's office. No matter. I knew that you were in Los Angeles, where you were not required, and that you ought to be in Stockholm, where you were not expected. If I had written direct to you, and asked you to come, you would certainly have treated it as a joke, especially as I could have given you no reasonable explanation—just then.

"But do you remember Mrs. Gregory at Los Angeles? Do you remember how often she turned the conversation latterly on the Copper House, what interest she showed in it, how she drew you on to give her such glowing descriptions of it that you began to feel quite home-sick? And how, by degrees, she inspired you with the idea of a voyage home, without further delay. Don't you remember all that?"

"Now you mention it—yes, I believe it really was that pretty Mrs. Gregory who put the journey into my head."

"You see, during my travels, I made friends in all sorts of places. There were you in Los Angeles; I ransacked my memory—ha! Mrs. Gregory!—

capital, an intelligent lady, a regular diplomat. I sent her an elaborate telegram. Can you forgive me?"

"My dear Mr. Wallion," replied Leo at once; "I am flattered, delighted! We must be friends now, and don't, whatever happens, spirit me back to California, before you have explained how I have become the object of such unbounded interest."

"In your capacity as owner of the Copper House."

"I haven't been a great success so far, in that line," remarked Leo. "When I tell you that I have been as good as turned out of it...."

He broke off his sentence in rather guilty confusion, at an unexpectedly piercing look from the other.

"Have you been there already, in spite of my warning?"

The young man nodded.

"And the immediate result is this nocturnal visit?" continued Wallion. "So you have been there? I was wondering all the time what could have happened to agitate you so much; I might have realized that you are one of those folks who never take advice.... Well, never mind, I am rather reluctant to take it myself, without knowing the reason for it. What did you see, to scare you so desperately?"

At this question, a sort of panic terror overwhelmed Leo. He saw once more the fugitive stumbling into the hall: he heard the shot ring out. He faltered: "I believe that a man has been killed—shot—at the Copper House; they didn't want me to see...."

Wallion bent down and looked into the young man's eyes, as a doctor would examine his patient.

"Tell me all about it," said he.

Leo thereupon poured out a very disjointed story, which the journalist heard in silence.

"You are sure that the girl called out 'Sergius'?"

"As sure as I am that Rastakov called the fugitive Bernard Jenin."

"And you think that Jenin certainly came into the house, but did not leave it again?"

"No, for it was impossible for him to get away."

"And you say that he disappeared altogether after that shot had been fired?"

"Yes, as though he had been instantaneously annihilated."

Wallion looked puzzled, and threw himself back in his chair with a gesture of vexation.

"Things don't tally! Talk of magic! I am brought up short whichever way I turn in this affair. Why should Lona Ivanovna shoot Bernard Jenin? —they ought...."

He scratched his head meditatively, and got up from his seat. "I know where I am with Rastakov, he is quite definitely on my black list. But Lona Ivanovna? and the girl who called out 'Sergius'?"

Presently Leo ventured to ask a question which had been on the tip of his tongue for a long time.

"I think it's my turn now to ask you for some light on these difficulties," said he; "you were joking, weren't you, when you said you needed my help?"

Wallion turned round and answered: "I suppose you know the Copper House like the palm of your hand?"

"Who should, if not I?"

"Exactly, you know the house, and you have the *right* to do so. Do you understand why these people want to buy the property? Simply to deprive you of that right. No one but yourself is in a position to know what is going on at the Copper House; and some underhand work is on foot there, which is bound to come to a head sooner or later. But I won't tantalize you with riddles, I will speak out."

He sat down again, and continued:

"It is a good thing you didn't run off to the police; that will come later, but not yet. I presume you did not meet Marcus Tassler?"

"No," replied Leo.

"That's just as well; it leaves us free to see the situation clearly."

"Excuse me," interrupted Leo, "I don't see anything clearly, as yet!"

"I am going to tell you a story," said Wallion. "Five months ago, I was sent for early one morning to see a dying man. I asked his name, and, to my surprise, I was given the name of a person who, several years previously, had been a friend of mine, and who had had the reputation of being a very promising journalist. But, in consequence of an extremely unfortunate and ridiculous love-affair, he went all to pieces, and finally disappeared, of his own accord, from our circle.

"I hastened to him, and found a poor, battered, neglected creature, lying, watch in hand, and speculating with a sort of childish curiosity, as to who would reach him first—myself or Death. They had told me beforehand that the unfortunate wretch had come home tipsy the night before, and had fallen out of a passage window on the fifth story, down to the stone pavement below. Everyone in the building had been aroused by the cry he uttered as he fell.

"I won't mention his name, for obvious reasons.

"When I came into the poverty-stricken bedroom, he raised his head from the pillow, and said very slowly and softly: 'I was afraid they wouldn't let you come!'

"I fancied he was delirious, and he looked as though he could barely have another minute to live.

"'Who do you mean?' I asked him.

"'The men who killed me,' was his reply.

"I hardly know what I said, for it was a dreadful shock to see the man whom I remembered full of life and health, lying an utter wreck before me. His back was broken. The change in him was so overwhelming that he could not but notice my consternation.

"'Yes, it is I,' he said, 'but in a minute or two I shall not be here any longer...quick, quick, bend down—no, do not touch my hand!' And he turned away his head, as though in shame.

"'Send away the doctor,' he murmured. I asked the doctor if he would remain outside the room until I called him, and stooped down over the dying man. His eyes glittered with fever, in his haggard, unshorn face. 'Do you know why I am dying?' said he. 'It's because I have seen too far into the depths of the Whirlpool...you are blind—all of you blind! Can you see nothing...?'

"He brought out these words with such an effort that it made him gasp for breath, and I gave him some water.

"'Mark my words,' he began again, in brief sentences and with repeated pauses. 'I have thrown away my own life...they bought me to do their work, but I won't...it is the beginning of Chaos...first in Russia...then it will spread everywhere...the man who dominates the Whirlpool is called Gabriel Ortiz; I found that out yesterday, and last night they killed me...for I am as good as dead already.'

"His failing energy beat out every word like the sparks from an anvil, and I listened breathlessly, for I realized that he was husbanding the last remnants of strength to make some amazing revelation.

"'Gabriel Ortiz...remember that name...his right hand is Baron Fayerling...but there are many others...their plan...it's appalling...the wild beast shall possess the earth!...'

"He groped for my hand, as though by clinging to me he could retain his hold on life a little longer. His anguish was fearful to see.

"'The War is nothing to what will happen, if Ortiz is not crushed...but be careful...they kill';...his voice grew fainter, and he lapsed into unconsciousness. I called in the doctor, but after a few minutes, he died.

"The dim room still seemed to echo with the sound of his voice. What was it he wanted to tell me?"

Wallion lighted a cigarette, and Leo could see that he was deeply moved.

"You see for yourself what a fantastic confession it appeared. And yet it never occurred to me to doubt the dead man's information, though I could find nothing to confirm it amongst his papers. But I made discreet inquiries of his neighbors, and when I went away, I was convinced that he had really been murdered by two men, who had lain in wait for him on the staircase, and pushed him through the window. I felt sure he had been in his right mind, but that he had been unable to complete a communication which would have been of incalculable importance."

"Could you find no clue to it?"

"No, but I took it for granted that he was the author of an article, headed: 'Who is the Man in the Whirlpool?' which had appeared a few weeks previously, in a little popular weekly paper. It proved impossible to verify it, because, for some unknown reason, the newspaper came to an end shortly after, and its contributors were all dispersed. In this remarkable article, attention was called to the fact that, during the War, Stockholm had become a center of activity for adventurers of a type hitherto unknown to civilization, and it was asserted that amongst them was a man who, as it were behind the back of the War, was organizing these mysterious forces, no one could say how or why.

"At all events, the writer of the article and the dying man took the same view, that something was brewing, and I had suspected as much already; things were going on in Stockholm which aroused my notice, there was a sort of subterranean movement which puzzled me. The image of a whirlpool was extraordinarily apt, and I could not doubt that the poor fellow I had just seen die, had been sucked into the vortex by sheer want, or by the temptation of easily earned money. Many weak and unfortunate characters have gone that way in these times! But what he caught sight of in the Whirlpool had evidently alarmed him, and he had made an effort to save his soul alive. Had I only arrived on the scene a few minutes earlier, I might have learned everything. At any rate, he had not summoned me in vain; I knew now that the Master Villain was called Gabriel Ortiz.

"But when I tried to obtain particulars as to this Gabriel Ortiz, I immediately met with the most extraordinary difficulties, which were in themselves a proof that he existed, but that he had safeguarded himself with the most intricate precautions. I had only just started my investigations in earnest, when the Russian Revolution broke out in March. At once I became aware, here in Stockholm, that under my very eyes, the sinister development was gaining strength. The Whirlpool was beginning to seethe. My attention had been directed towards Baron Fayerling, but I had not succeeded in discovering anything mysterious about him. He stays at one of the best hotels, goes everywhere, and lives officially on the rents of his Roumanian property. But as Roumanian property is just now a very uncertain source of income, Baron Fayerling also does business of the most up-to-date kind, and has associated himself for this purpose with Marcus

Tassler, the manager of the Finno-Russian Import and Export Company, a thorough going profiteer, and even outside business matters a regular shark.

"Meanwhile, the odd thing about Tassler is the interest he takes in the Copper House. Mark this: we have at the Copper House three perfectly inconspicuous persons, who seem to prefer living in the most complete retirement; they are Andrei Bernin, his sister and his daughter. As long as I have had my eye on them, they have never left the Copper House, and have not evinced any particular friendship for Tassler or the baron, who often stay there as self-invited guests. Tassler has shown unremitting interest in the Copper House, and it is he who has brought about, first the lease of the entire property, and now the liberal offer to purchase it. He has installed there a staff of attendants, whom he commands with almost military zeal. The gate-keeper is called Tugan; no one knows his nationality, but he is a regular watchdog, and only too glad to get food, drink and fighting, provided gratis. He, of course, lives at the lodge.

"Then we have the gardener, whom you have probably not seen yet; his name is Rosenthal, a taciturn, meditative sort of fellow, with something refined about him which distinguishes him slightly from the rest. He has two underlings, and these three live in the gardener's cottage behind the big house.

"Next we have the cowhouse and the stable, which now contain only three cows and two horses—but four cowherds and two grooms are kept to look after them—what do you make of that?

"Wait! The list is not complete yet. There are the six men whom Sonia Bernin calls the forest-guards, and they really *do* keep watch in the wood, as you can testify from personal experience!

"And finally, two individuals are installed at the little cottage beside the pier that runs out into the Bay; they fish, and sail in and out of the farther islands, but what they catch, neither you nor I can say!

"So there we have a retinue of eighteen men—but not a trace of either men or women servants in the Copper House itself. Not counting the three Bernins, who are Russians, everyone else in the place is a foreigner, although ten or eleven of them can speak Swedish, and six have been naturalized as Swedish citizens."

"And you said you didn't know the Copper House!" exclaimed Leo; "why, you know it better than I do!"

"Anybody can find out that sort of thing," replied Wallion. "There is no secret about it. But the burning question is: what is *really* going on at the Copper House?"

CHAPTER VII

The Slayers

"Let us try and see exactly how we stand," went on the Problem-hunter; "up to now there has been a lot of vague talk about whirlpools, chaos, wild beasts, and the like. Accurately speaking, we already have a complete chain, with the Copper House at one end, and the mysterious Gabriel Ortiz at the other. Two of the most important links in the chain are Fayerling and Tassler. I might add a third: Rastakov, though he is a subordinate, a sort of non-commissioned officer, so to speak, who gets all the dirty jobs for his share. Now we will take this extraordinary 'chain,' link by link, and sum up all we know about it. Of its head, Ortiz, we are not yet in a position to say anything very definite; most of our information about him dates from ten years back."

Wallion proceeded to give a brief outline of the story which he had related to B.22, a few hours earlier.

"Baron Fayerling, the fashionable society man, with his Roumanian property, is the next on our list," he continued; "he manages to invest his money on the most extraordinarily favorable terms. He banks with no fewer than six banks in Stockholm, two in Göteburg, and one in Copenhagen, Malmö, Christiania, and Hälsingfors respectively.

"The grand total of his outstanding account rises and falls in a very peculiar way: at the beginning of February he had no less than 12,000,000 kroner, at the end of the same month only half that amount, and at the end of March only a paltry 100,000. Two weeks later, he paid in on one day, 1,000,000 kroner to every one of his banking accounts, making another sum of 12,000,000 kroner. And now, in July, his account has reached the enormous total of over 20,000,000 kroner. Whatever kind of business does he carry on? No one can say. I have myself verified the names of eighty-four different persons, who have cashed the baron's checks; of these, all except four were foreigners, and half of them left Sweden afterwards, mostly bound for Russia or Finland. This influx of people, all of whom received money, and sometimes a great deal of it, from Fayerling, was largest at the beginning of March. Each man paid a short visit to the baron's room at the hotel, and two of them were shadowed the whole time by Rastakov. Three of them went out to the Copper House.

"We mustn't forget to mention Tassler, whose interests are closely allied to those of the baron. The Finno-Russian Import and Export Company is a bona fide concern; you can go whenever you like to their office in Drottning Street, and negotiate the buying or selling of almost any conceivable thing, for, like most other modern business men, Tassler deals in practically any goods, from clinical thermometers to coffee, tea and cocoa. A small number of the articles in which they deal are only to be found in the catalogue, but this is probably due to the fact that their value fluctuates with the continual rise of prices.

"Tassler's banking-accounts are as unimpeachable as those of the baron, and are deposited in much the same way. In one or two cases, I have ascertained that these two men had concluded a deal in which there was a genuine exchange of cash and goods; but, on the whole, I have not been able to discover that the Agents of the Company, who are to be found in all the large Scandinavian towns, carry on any business beyond an incessant correspondence, on the firm's stamped writing paper, with Messrs. Tassler and Fayerling.

"I have read through a whole pile of such letters; they are full of lists of goods, and business terms. Sometimes if it is anything urgent, they send telegrams. Tassler's agent in Göteburg did so when you landed from the American vessel. One gets the impression of elaborate machinery in full working-order, but it is not so easy to ascertain its object, for, if it were to make money, Fayerling and Tassler would not have a rag to their backs by this time.

"To put the thing in a nutshell, we see two gentlemen who allow millions to flow out through a hundred different channels, but we search in vain for the source of these millions or for the ultimate aim of such lavish expenditure. If it were a question of the usual spy-business, it would be easily understood, but neither Fayerling nor Tassler nor any of their associates in and around the Copper House appear to have the slightest connection with the belligerent powers. No, there is something else in the wind— but what?

"When I began my investigations, I evolved two different theories. The first was, that this was an organization for gun-running. It was a fact that Fayerling had been somehow implicated in the infamously famous expedition which attempted to smuggle explosives across the northern boundary into Finland, but was quashed by the Swedish authorities, and its promoters mysteriously dispersed. The equally famous motor-launch 'Nelly,' which attempted to cross the Gulf of Bothnia with a cargo of modern rifles, was seen a week previously cruising off the Copper House. But I could not obtain sufficient proof; and, above all, I was soon convinced that neither of such incidents could be more than a detail, a mere trifle, in Fayerling's daily program. I could see that he only goes in for big things. Thereupon, I started a fresh theory: that the whole affair was a federation to assist various political fugitives and conspirators in the technical part of their plans, such as forging passports, protecting them against counter-espionage, financing their journeys, purchasing weapons…in short, a kind of revolutionary stock-jobbery. As a matter of fact, hundreds of revolutionaries and the like, with weapons and 'red' literature, were smuggled into Russia by way of Stockholm, at the beginning of this year. It would certainly be an interesting interpretation of the activities of the Finno-Russian Import and Export Company!

"But that explanation proved inadequate also: its aims were far too limited. Fayerling and Tassler were obviously interested in the Russian Revolution, but even after a revolutionary Government came into power in Petrograd, their mysterious work continued with unabated vigor, directed by the still invisible Gabriel Ortiz. I felt quite at a loss….

"Then, all of a sudden, a period of inactivity set in; it started some weeks ago. No more streams of unknown visitors, no more of that colossal expenditure…absolute stagnation! I noticed that Fayerling was beginning to get fidgety; about once a day, usually rather late, he would hold a long conversation on the telephone, after which he regularly countermanded certain orders, and substituted new ones. I felt sure that Ortiz must be at the other end of the line during these talks, but I found it impossible to verify this. It was soon evident that some new plan was afoot, and I determined to redouble my watchfulness. One day my assistant, Robert Lang, overheard in the street a conversation between the baron and Tassler in which the latter alluded several times to 'Tarraschin's memorandum.' This gave us a fresh idea.

"Do you know what 'Tarraschin's memorandum' is?

"It has only once been referred to publicly, and that was by a Bulgarian journalist, who had got into some trouble over a newspaper controversy. He referred to 'Tarraschin's memorandum' as 'a bomb which, if it came into the right hands, would annihilate Europe.' The document must have been drawn up in Moscow immediately after the March revolution, and Prince Tarraschin was the originator of it. It contained a complete plan to destroy the Revolution and reinstate the Tsar, and practically all the best-known names of the Russian 'ancien régime' would be irrevocably compromised if the document came to light. Strangely enough, or perhaps, naturally enough, Prince Tarraschin died at the end of March, before his plan had gone further than the paper on which it was written, and the whole thing seemed to have died out altogether.

"This is where Bernard Jenin comes in, and at the same moment, Fayerling's attitude of suspense ends as though by magic! I see a person, simply known as B.22, told off to escort Jenin; I see Rastakov keeping an eye on them both; earnest consultations take place in the baron's apartments. To my surprise, I learn that this Bernard Jenin is in possession of nothing less than the Tarraschin document, and I gather that there is a plot to rob him of it.

"Then, having for a month past played the silent part of an unseen spectator, I decide to step in!

"I saw Rastakov go straight from the baron's room to that of Jenin, and I put a spoke in his wheel. I warned Jenin to look out carefully for a better hiding-place, and safer friends; he hardly said a word, but simply vanished. I wondered which way he had gone, but I could not follow him, because it became necessary for me, once for all, to take up a definite attitude as regarded the baron. I now learn for the first time, that Jenin dashed off to the Copper House, that Rastakov promptly followed him, and that they have, in all probability, murdered him there."

* * * *

Maurice Wallion told his story rapidly, and almost without a pause. The silence which succeeded it lasted so long that it began to get on Leo's nerves. It seemed to him as though the mere fact of having listened to this fantastic tale brought with it some sort of responsibility—an awakening sense of duty.

"Do you think, too, that Jenin is dead?" he asked, just to break the silence.

"One can think anything, when one knows nothing," replied Wallion gravely. "I would rather have no theory than one which can be proved to have no foundation. But that Jenin, as soon as I have rescued him from one danger should run straight into another—that he should turn up so apparently unnecessarily at the Copper House, right in the middle of the hornets' nest, seems so senseless, that Lona Ivanovna's revolver-shot only puts the finishing touch to the story! The only thing that really puzzles me is why Sonia Bernin should have cried out: 'Sergius!'"

"Where do you suppose Tarraschin's document can have got to now?"

"Possibly into Lona Ivanovna's, or more accurately, into Andrei Bernin's hands. At any rate, Rastakov did not get hold of it."

"How can you be sure of that?"

"In this way: if he had been able yesterday to report the discovery of the document to the baron, and he in his turn to Ortiz, they would have not made such a frantic search amongst all my belongings later in the evening. They would have held all the trumps in their hands, and would have considered me comparatively harmless. But instead of that, they have turned my room at the office topsy-turvy, and have tried to do the same thing here, to find that paper, and that assures me that Rastakov has not discovered it at the Copper House—yet!"

"That seems probable," Leo agreed; "so you knew how they had ransacked your office?"

"Yes, Robert Lang telephoned it. But they carried off nothing more important than a photograph of Sonia Bernin."

"They didn't even get that!" cried Leo, triumphantly. "Look what I have! I got there first!"

There was such simple pride in the young man's look and words, that the Problem-hunter burst out laughing, and gave him a hearty slap on the back.

"Ah, now you are playing tricks on me," said he; "it's the Finger of Destiny, or the Master Mind, or whatever else you like to call it. It is quite evident that we two must coöperate!"

"Yes, we *must* do something," declared Leo, who had certainly never shown himself so decided in the whole of his life. "I am glad you summoned me home from California. We mustn't let things slide: we must keep a sharp look-out on what is going on at the Copper House."

The Problem-hunter looked pleasantly surprised at the reiterated "we must," and began to think that this young fellow had something in him after all.

"You heard what I said about Ortiz," said he warningly. "Don't imagine that the Man in the Whirlpool is a myth, and can be abolished in half an hour. He exists, and he is dangerous."

"Dangerous!" exclaimed Leo, coloring a little in his excitement. "With you to back me, who can call a man from the other side of the world, without saying a word to him! I know nothing of Ortiz, but at any rate, he has got you for an enemy!"

It was plain to see that the young man, like almost all those who met Wallion, had surrendered unconditionally to his suggestive personality. The calm voice and the keen eyes inspired Leo with unlimited confidence, and, at this moment, his mobile, rather undecided face took on a look of the journalist's, with his determined mouth and chin.

Wallion, who was watching him, took up his tumbler quickly to hide a smile, and said: "Unfortunately, though we know nothing about Ortiz, he knows all about us. He has the advantage of us there. But he and his satellites are suffering from one drawback: there are too many of them. 'A chain is no stronger than its weakest link.'"

"And it's just that link we have got to find," cried Leo.

"Yes, that's exactly what I was trying to do yesterday afternoon, while I was keeping Fayerling's counterspies at arm's length. I found that the man we know under the pseudonym of B.22, who escorted Bernard Jenin to Stockholm, has in some way incurred the baron's suspicions. I profited by this, and managed to fall in with B.22."

Here the journalist looked at his watch, and broke off: "I say, how time has flown! It is past six already!"

He extinguished the lamp, and they could see a glimmer of daylight between the thick curtains, which he now flung open. Waves of bright sunshine streamed into the room, and when the window was opened a refreshing morning-breeze blew softly in on their heated faces. They both inhaled it with enjoyment, and Wallion said: "Another day! I wonder if Gabriel Ortiz slept last night—not without dreaming, I'll wager. As long as there is a doubt about Tarraschin's memorandum…but who knows, everything may be cleared up in an hour's time!"

"Why are you looking out into the street?"

"To see if the house is watched."

"And is it?"

"Fortunately not. We are lucky."

"How odd you look! One might think you were waiting for somebody. What's up?"

"I am expecting B.22. He was to be here at about seven."

Leo jumped up. "B.22 coming here?"

"Yes, the poor chap is scared stiff, and is inclined to betray Ortiz to save his own skin. I have promised to help him, as soon as he has made a full confession, though I doubt whether he will prove a very creditable witness…."

The door-bell rang; Wallion went to answer it, and a man came in hurriedly, holding a newspaper in his hand. It was the young journalist, Robert Lang, and he was so much out of breath that he could not speak for a minute, but handed the paper to his Chief with a silent gesture.

"You are out early," remarked Wallion coolly, though he already guessed the truth.

"No," retorted Lang hastily, "say rather, too late! Wallion, they have forestalled us again—B.22 is dead!"

"Dead!" echoed Leo and the Problem-hunter together. The latter, to whom Lang had handed the paper, glanced through it, and came to an underlined paragraph, which he read aloud:

"Sudden Death in the Street Last Night

"About eleven o'clock last night, a middle-aged and rather poorly dressed man was found dead upon one of the benches in the Railway Park. The man, who was apparently one of the many unknown strangers who are so frequently to be met with in Stockholm at the present time, seems to have died quite suddenly, no doubt in consequence of a heart-attack. Nothing was found in his pockets, except a card upon which was written in red ink, 'B.22.' It is therefore impossible to identify him. He was dressed...."

A brief description followed. Wallion threw down the paper and asked:

"Is the *Morning Post* the only paper that gives the news?"

"Yes," replied Lang; "it must have been one of their reporters who came across him."

"Have you verified the report?"

"Yes, the dead man is B.22, there's no doubt about that."

"No," said Wallion slowly; "no doubt about it. We might have expected it. Poor wretch! The Whirlpool has sucked him in!"

"He makes the third," said Leo, looking much disturbed. "We *must* give notice to the police now!"

Wallion, who was standing with his head bent, now looked up.

"The third, if Bernard Jenin is really dead," he said. "But how can the police help us? What's the good of bringing an accusation against one Gabriel Ortiz, when no one has any idea where to find him? Or to arrest Fayerling or Tassler, against whom we have not a shadow of proof? Or to tell the fantastic history of Tarraschin's memorandum which none of us has seen? Go to the police, if you like—and in a week's time we shall be scoffed at as the most arrant liars and slanderers in Europe, and that is saying a good deal in this year of grace 1917!"

"But—aren't we right?" asked Leo, amazed.

"We haven't the *right* to be right, as long as we can't *prove* that we are! And you see, they have robbed us of our proof before we could take advantage of it."

"What shall we do, then?"

The Problem-hunter's gray eyes began to sparkle with indomitable energy. He spoke rapidly, but in such a tone that every word was impressed upon their minds.

"Lang, you go straight off to Lawyer Burchardt as soon as his office is open, and inform him on Mr. Grath's behalf that the Copper House is not for sale. You may tell the lawyer, under the seal of secrecy, as much of the truth as is necessary. After that, wait for further instructions from me."

Robert Lang looked at Leo.

"Yes," said he quickly; "it's quite correct, I have no intention of selling the Copper House to those people."

"And you, Mr. Grath," continued Wallion, "are presumed to be locked up in your bedroom at the present minute, fast asleep at the Copper House. It's a grand position, at the very center of all that's going on. So, catch the first train out to Karkby, and get back to your room the same way you left it—as long as nobody sees you doing it!"

Leo drew a deep breath.

"But supposing anyone saw me in Stockholm last night?"

"Nobody would have dreamed that you would be here, and that fellow outside my door had quite enough to do to look after himself."

"And what about you? what are you going to do?"

"I am coming with you to the Copper House!"

Part II—The Twentieth of July

CHAPTER VIII

Lona Ivanovna Asks Her First Question

When a house is guarded with such infinite precaution as was the case with the Copper House, it becomes, as Wallion expressed it, "a pleasantly exciting adventure" to enter it by broad daylight, without being seen.

By his advice, they had quitted the train one station beyond Karkby, and gone the rest of the way on foot, through the wood. They crossed the southern boundary as an invading army crosses the border of a hostile country: by forced marches, and with intense caution.

As soon as they reached the top of the hill, they could see at some distance through the trees, the massive roof of copper which was their goal. The sun shone brightly in the still atmosphere; no smoke issued as yet from the chimneys of the great house; the unploughed field in front of it lay bare and desolate. But, on looking to the left, they caught sight of a man sitting motionless upon a stone at the outskirts of the wood, with his face turned towards the field, and a gun between his knees. It was one of the forest-guards.

"We seem to be in luck," murmured Wallion.

"Luck!" echoed Leo irritably. "They are watching the path and we shall not be able to go a hundred steps without being seen...."

"Just so. It is lucky that they are watching the Copper House *so openly*. If we had not found that sentry posted there, I should have felt uneasy, for it would certainly mean that your escapade last night had been discovered, and a trap laid. But now they are keeping guard as they always do, and we can go happily on."

Wallion moved forward, but Leo pulled him back by the coat.

"What are you going to do?" he whispered.

"To make a flanking movement," replied the Problem-hunter.

They skirted the hill behind the sentry, and approached the avenue by slow degrees. Suddenly Wallion halted.

"There's another of them!" he whispered.

They could see another armed man some way beyond them; like the first, he was staring idly at the field, and they heard him yawn loudly, after which he filled and lighted his pipe; the smell of tobacco was wafted up to them.

"Look, they are waking up in the Copper House," whispered Leo.

Smoke was rising from one of the chimneys, and the Problem-hunter gazed critically at it, remarking:

"In twenty minutes' time, they will knock at your door to tell you that breakfast is ready."

"They are bound to find out directly that I am not there," answered Leo quickly; "we can't possibly get in now without being seen."

"Where there's a will, there's a way! We'll try, at all events."

Wallion spoke with irresistible decision, and Leo dared not protest. They passed, at some distance, a third sentry, and were now close to the avenue, and about half-way up it. The huge trees formed a sort of roof above them, and the trunks bordered the path like a fourfold row of dark, massive pillars. Wallion looked all round.

"That's our best way," said he: "come along."

"The avenue?" said Leo.

"Yes, where else? Why go in by the back way, when we can arrive in style, sheltered by these great trees? Remember that they keep a look-out on the avenue from the porter's lodge, and anyone seeing us here will take it for granted that we belong to the house. Forward!"

He took Leo by the arm, and began to walk up the avenue.

"Step out," he said smiling. "They see us now, but they aren't paying us any attention."

It was difficult to say whether any of the three sentries whom they had just passed, and had now left on their right, took the slightest notice of the two men in the avenue; at all events, they raised no alarm, though Leo, hardly daring to breathe, expected them to do so at any minute.

Wallion moved softly and swiftly, as though making for some definite point, and Leo followed him as best he could; five minutes later they made a half-turn to the left, and saw the Copper House straight in front of them.

"Which is the window of your room?" whispered Wallion.

"On the north side, second floor, hidden by the trees. I have climbed up the spout to that window any number of times in my life, without being caught...."

"I fancy we shall manage it again now," remarked Wallion, but at the same instant he pulled Leo back among the bushes.

Somebody was coming. Steps crunched on the gravel, and a man passed quite close. Presently they crept out of their hiding-place, and saw the person, who had gone by without suspecting their proximity, mount the terrace-steps, and disappear in the direction of the house. They both recognized Rastakov. While they still hesitated to advance any further, they heard his steps again; he had gone the round of the house and was now standing on the terrace. They dared not raise their heads, for his face was turned their way. They could hear him light a cigarette, and the next few seconds seemed interminable. Then the glass door leading to the hall opened with a crash, and a harsh voice said:

"Maxim Rastakov!"

"What is it, Lona Ivanovna?"

"Allow me to tell you, Rastakov, that if you don't turn out that filthy tramp who is sitting in the kitchen, and the miserable object who stands and yawns in the hall, I shall do it myself."

"Not yet, my good Lona Ivanovna; not until you tell me where I can find Bernard Jenin."

"Haven't you searched the whole house? Do you think I have hidden him in one of these drawers? You needn't make faces; you are quite ugly enough as it is...."

Rastakov laughed.

"Lona Ivanovna," said he, "go upstairs and wake the young fellow who fancies that he owns this house, and see that he comes out here without noticing anything. We can talk about Bernard Jenin afterwards."

"Don't I tell you that he has gone!"

"Yes, I haven't a doubt of it! He's gone, but *the matter doesn't end there*! When you can show me *how Bernard Jenin disappeared*, I will remove those men. But only on one condition: mind that the blue light appears every evening."

There was something ominous in the cold, clear tones of Rastakov's voice, which made Leo's blood run cold. A pause followed. Then the old lady said, as harshly as before, but with rising anger in her voice:

"See to the blue light yourself, Rastakov. Perhaps it may show up your face in its proper setting, and let people see what a scoundrel you are!"

"They have realized that already, Lona Ivanovna, and that is why they make use of me."

He laughed again loudly, went down the steps of the terrace, and disappeared down the avenue. The glass door slammed again, and all was still.

Wallion sprang up, pulling Leo with him.

"Quick, quick," he whispered; "now we know how the land lies; they are keeping watch indoors, and your absence last night has not been discovered. Quick, to your room."

They could see above them the open window of Leo's bedroom, and without more ado, Wallion climbed with noiseless agility up the copper spout, and swung himself over the window-sill.

Leo followed him with greater difficulty, for, in his nervous excitement, his heart was beating so rapidly that it made him feel faint and breathless.

"Here we are, at last!" said the Problem-hunter, seating himself on a chair, and taking stock of his surroundings; "an uncommonly jolly little room! Give me some idea as quickly as you can, of the geography of the house, so that I may know how to find my way about it."

But this was asking too much. Leo had thrown himself speechless on the bed, and did not answer. Wallion looked at him more closely, and saw that he was shivering as though with cold, and that beads of perspiration stood on his forehead.

"Look here, you must keep those nerves of yours in better order! Yes, I know neither of us had a wink of sleep last night, but you will feel another man when you have had a splash in cold water, and changed your things: do it now!"

"I left my luggage at Stockholm," murmured Leo, without moving. "But it doesn't matter...."

"Well then, take a nip out of my pocket-pistol," said his friend, perseveringly. "There, you see, you're better already."

And, in fact, Leo sat up, after a mouthful from Wallion's silver flask.

"What's the good?" asked the young man slowly. "Now we are here, after so much trouble, it seems to me we can't do anything. If we stop where we are, we shall be no better than prisoners, and who knows what may happen when they discover that you are here? We have voluntarily deprived ourselves of liberty...."

"No," replied the journalist decidedly; "we have gained it. Full, unlimited liberty to be in the very place where they least want us. They will do all in their power to get us out of it. I say 'us,' because they will not remain long in ignorance of my presence here, although several things will probably happen first."

"No doubt about that. There will be plenty of movement—but as for liberty—that's quite another matter!"

"Don't misunderstand me," said the Problem-hunter, with a steely glint in his eye. "In Stockholm I was obliged to keep a constant look-out, to try and discover my opponents; here, I can see enemies freely on every side of me, and may expect a fresh one at any minute. The situation is perfectly simple—we have only to be prepared!"

"Are you armed?"

"Of course! I have a perfect arsenal, what with a pair of eyes, two ears, a tongue, and my brains. Don't you think that's enough? Well, here's a revolver into the bargain. That will do for Rastakov."

"Or for Lona Ivanovna, who shot Bernard Jenin!" exclaimed Leo impetuously. "You may joke, but I...."

The journalist came and sat down beside him.

"Why, now you are angry," he said calmly; "that's good, it shows you're in working order again."

Nobody could resist Maurice Wallion when he chose. Leo began to smile.

A soft breeze from the wooded hills around them blew in upon them, cooling and refreshing: a blue butterfly was fluttering in the folds of the white window-curtains.

"How can I be angry!" said Leo. "But you are so—different from other people. Here we have just smuggled ourselves into a house which is full of mysteries, and probably of powerful enemies as well, and you sit down and deal in paradoxes. You are playing with danger!"

"My dear fellow," replied the journalist, "when one has got to the point of playing with danger, it means that one has first learned to estimate it correctly. A hunter does not judge of the strength of a lion merely by shooting it. He tracks it to its lair, 'plays' it, so to speak—and in that way forms a true estimate of its individual powers."

"Stop, stop!" entreated Leo, holding up his hands in mock surrender. "You will be making me say next, that Rastakov is my dearest friend!"

"And you couldn't do a wiser thing," retorted the journalist imperturbably. "The wind would be quite taken out of his sails, and he would become wax in your hands."

He bent forward, and added impressively:

"What you *must* do—and now I am speaking quite seriously—is to be a really staunch friend to Lona Ivanovna and Sonia Bernin."

"What about Andrei Bernin?"

"I intend to befriend him myself, for a reason that will probably surprise you both. But now it is time for you to go downstairs."

* * * *

A quarter of an hour later, Leonard Grath came down into the hall. Sure enough, there by the glass door sat a man, his gun propped against the wall, within easy reach; he got up as soon as he saw Leo, and stood at attention. The young man went past him into the dining-room, where he could hear low voices. The breakfast table was laid near the windows, and with some surprise, he realized that they were waiting for him.

Sonia Bernin was standing by the window, and when she turned and saw him, she greeted him with a friendly smile. Lona Ivanovna, who had been talking in a low and impressive tone, also turned round. Leo bowed. As a self-invited guest, he found the situation a little awkward, but his hostess said frankly:

"Good morning, Mr. Grath. I am afraid we left you very unceremoniously yesterday evening, but I trust you will remember that a place will always be laid for you as long as you give us the pleasure of your company."

"It is most kind of you," mumbled Leo. He noticed for the first time that the old blind author was also in the room. Andrei Bernin was sitting in an armchair, stiff and upright, in a listening attitude, near a window on the left, with the curtains drawn. In his dim corner at the end of the room, he looked like some grotesque and inanimate mask, with his white beard, blue spectacles, and black velvet skull-cap: a pathetic and immovable figure, laid aside and forgotten. As Lona Ivanovna's masculine profile and vigorous form bent over the blind man, the contrast was so acute, that Leo could not help feeling touched by it.

"Andrei Ivanovitch," said his sister, "this is Mr. Grath."

"I'm very glad to make your acquaintance, sir," said Leo.

The blind man bowed, and held out a thin, but white and well-kept hand.

"We are all glad that you have come," said he, in a voice as low and gentle as a softly tinkling bell. "But why have you come alone?"

After a pause, during which Sonia raised her head and looked at Leo, the blind man repeated his question, still more slowly and mechanically.

"Why have you come alone?"

Lona Ivanovna also cast an inquiring glance at the young man. The blind man had clutched the arms of his chair and was bending forward; little wrinkles undulated over his worn face, and the blue spectacles gleamed like two steel mirrors. Leo, whose thoughts were centered on the journalist hidden in his bedroom, felt like a prisoner at the bar.

"I am certainly alone," he said slowly, "though I didn't come alone."

"Ah, indeed," said the blind man, in a tone which suddenly resembled his sister's. "Not alone? And who was your companion?"

"He was a stranger to me," explained Leo. "Bernard Jenin was my traveling companion in the train yesterday."

The expression of the faces around him changed suddenly, and became cold, strange, and secretive. It seemed almost as though the sunny atmosphere of the room was charged with electricity, which sent a shock through him, and a new light dawned upon him. He perceived that these three persons were unhappy, weighed down by an unknown catastrophe, or by the apprehension of an imminent one. He had been cruel: he had reopened a wound. They were looking at him as though they saw in him an executioner, and Sonia's eyes were misty with tears. The old man's voice broke the silence:

"We mustn't judge by appearances. Important conclusions are often based on very slight grounds. And although I cannot see you, I can feel what you are thinking. The question is, whether Bernard Jenin is still in the Copper House, or whether Lona Ivanovna killed him last night, at sunset."

Leo raised his hand involuntarily, and took a step back. The blind man, who sat with his white head turned towards him, continued softly:

"What, are you afraid of your own suspicions? At sunset, that's a good time to die! Why do you let the matter trouble you so deeply? There are so many brave fellows, a hundred times better than Bernard Jenin, who are lying dead in a hell of carnage, that it seems almost a luxury to die of nothing worse than one little revolver-shot."

"Mr. Bernin!" burst out Leo violently, "I have not expressed any such suspicion!"

"No, *I* have expressed it. To banish a groundless suspicion it is often enough just to put it into words. Some thoughts won't stand that proof. You said you saw Bernard Jenin in the train, and you have guessed that a mystery attaches to his arrival here. But why need the mystery be a criminal one? Why must you feel obliged to extort an explanation which would be willingly given to you, if it were possible?"

Leo did not hesitate a moment. The frank words acted upon him like a fresh breeze, blowing away the cobwebs, and he exclaimed: "I will not insist upon any explanation. You do not know me; I cannot claim to be your friend, but at any rate, do not regard me as your enemy."

Lona Ivanovna had crossed her lean arms upon her breast and she laughed grimly. It struck Leo how much alike Andrei Bernin and his sister were, in spite of their outward dissimilarity. The same quiet and resigned manner, the same intellectual strength, characterized them both. He could not understand how he had seen in the blind author nothing more than a weak and senile invalid.

"Well, well!" said the old lady, "I see that we are agreed. So let us have breakfast."

The tension was eased, though a certain amount of constraint still remained. Only Leo and Sonia Bernin exchanged a few commonplace remarks every now and then.

As soon as they got up from the table, the elder lady took out her interminable crochet, as if it was the only thing that mattered; then she leaned over the table, looked the young man straight in the face, and inquired:

"When is Maurice Wallion coming?"

"I—I can't say," answered Leo, taken by surprise. "Why do you ask me?"

"Because, if he has a mind to rescue Bernard Jenin a second time, he has my permission to be quick about it!"

Leo was tempted to tell the truth about the journalist's hiding-place, but he contented himself with answering: "I am convinced that he will come—but he will choose his own time."

CHAPTER IX

Unrest in Both Camps: an Outpost Skirmish and a Warning

It was raining in Stockholm: heavy clouds were drifting over the sky, and an occasional peal of thunder rolled over the wet, glistening roofs. At the office of the Finno-Russian Import and Export Company, Marcus Tassler stood looking gloomily out at the rain. He was alone in the two showily-furnished rooms, for he had sent out the typist who was his only assistant, if one excepts those who came and went on business that had nothing to do with the purchase and sale of tea and coffee. He was alone with his thoughts, hence his gloom.

He was thinking principally of the baron—who had inspired him with a certain amount of dread that morning—and of the future, which he dreaded even more. He was aware that he was standing on dangerous ground, and he knew that his one hope of escape was—in plain English—to cut and run! That is an unpleasant conviction for anyone, and especially for a man whose most prominent characteristics are an oriental love of pleasure and a barbaric thirst for gold.

Marcus Tassler gulped down half a glass of old cognac, and lighted a dark cigar, with a band round it. He looked at that minute like some fat, pagan high-priest, engaged in mystic rites, and in forecasting gruesome omens from the sacrificial offerings.

Baron Fayerling came in without knocking. He greeted his partner with a diabolical smile, provoked partly by Tassler's harassed expression, partly by his empty glass. He appeared to be in a hurry, for he kept his hat on, and remained standing, leaning on his cane.

"Well!" said Tassler sharply. "You are late. Have you caught him?"

"No," replied the baron. "That duffer I sent up to his flat last night, came back in a panic, reporting that the journalist was at home, and had a visitor into the bargain—since then, Maurice Wallion has vanished as completely as Pharaoh in the Red Sea."

"Does nobody know who his visitor was?"

"No."

"And when our men searched his room at the office, did they find nothing?"

"No. Nothing! Nichts! Rien!"

The baron uttered each successive negative with an explosive emphasis which made his companion wince. He added:

"His being away wouldn't matter so much if I had not the written proof that the fellow is set on exterminating us. Can you imagine anything cooler than his treatment of Rastakov and myself! Informing us frankly that he will fight us for the Tarraschin document—for, of course, that's what he is after."

"At any rate, he can't get anything now out of B.22," remarked Tassler.

"Out of whom?" said the baron sharply. "What may B.22 be? I'm not acquainted with the witness."

"Oh, come, baron, between ourselves! From the way in which he died, I can pretty well guess whom you sent...."

The baron collared the fat man, and shook him till he quivered like a jelly.

"Idiot!" he cried. "You will chatter your head off some day! We don't speak about dead men."

When the baron loosed his hold, Tassler filled and drained his glass once more; his hands were trembling, and his eyes wandered uneasily round the room.

"I don't like that business with B.22," he muttered. "What's the sense of employing persons whom one has to kill as soon as they get to know anything? The Chief said nothing about murder, when we first discussed our plans."

"Nonsense. In such an undertaking as ours, there must always come a time, sooner or later, when we can stick at nothing. But that's no business of yours. Have you been to see Burchardt?"

"Yes, I have been to him."

Tassler thrust his hands into his trouser-pockets, and confronted the baron.

"Yes, *I have* seen the damned lawyer! Fayerling, they *mean* to fight us: there is something up. Maurice Wallion is at the back of it, devil take him!"

His bloodshot eyes turned towards the glass, but he abstained, and went on with dry lips:

"That Burchardt is a fox. He looked at me quite differently when I came in and was twice as obliging as he had been before. I mistrust people who grow politer the better one knows them! He was ready to lick my boots! I thought everything was going smoothly, and I was saying that as I had heard that the owner of the Copper House was in town, and the matter was urgent—when suddenly, the old rascal, who had been listening to me without turning a hair, said, quite softly:

"'Mr. Grath has changed his mind. He is not thinking of selling the Copper House, before he has gone into the matter thoroughly.' I can tell you, I nearly fell off my chair: 'Not sell!' 'No, very sorry—old traditions—family inheritance,' and all the rest of it. To hell with the old traditions! They are on our track, Fayerling, they mean to 'go into the matter thoroughly!'"

Tassler almost groaned as he said these words, but after a minute, he glanced at the baron with the humiliated surprise of a story-teller who sees his best point fall flat; the baron looked perfectly unconcerned.

"So they decline to sell," said he, slowly. "I guessed as much. Leonard Grath is at the Copper House, and no doubt he has been warned by Wallion. You are right, we are in for a fight."

"Fayerling, Tarraschin's memorandum will be the ruin of us!"

"It would, if we were all as blind and as cowardly as you. Can't you understand that no human beings ever had greater luck than we had, when Bernard Jenin, contrary to all expectation, fled for refuge to the Copper House."

"But Rastakov couldn't get hold of him!"

"We have to thank the old she-grenadier for that. Andrei Bernin and his sister evidently mean to play for their own hand, but I intend to smoke out that wasp's nest—the Bernins won't be of any more use to us. Of course, Bernard Jenin counted on their help, although Lona Ivanovna seems to have played the wrong card. Oh well, the document is there, at any rate, as safe as though it were in a strong-box...."

"Who is Bernard Jenin really?"

"How should I know? A knave or a fool. You have heard that in Moscow he went by the name of Doctor Zero, and he managed to get the document from our agent, who was on the point of bringing it here. At first I thought it was all up, but thank goodness, Jenin was idiot enough to travel direct to Stockholm, and had B.22 at his elbow during the whole journey: he simply had him on a string! And, not content with coming to Stockholm, no sooner had that journalist rescued him from room 23, than the silly fool runs straight off to the Copper House. And then you come and say that we have no luck!"

Tassler sucked away at his cigar with his thick lips: his eyes looked like two china marbles.

"Can I see his photograph?" he asked in a hesitating voice. Fayerling threw it down in front of him, without a word.

One might have thought that Tassler was afraid of the picture: he held it at arm's length, between his thumb and finger, whilst a curiously fixed expression came over his face; he felt as though an electric shock had gone through him, and he tottered slightly.

"You must be drunk!" said the baron, with cold disapproval; but this diagnosis, though founded on past experience, and supported by the witness of the empty glass, was incorrect. Marcus Tassler was perfectly sober, though his legs were giving away under him, and his brain was spinning like a Catherine wheel. He sat down.

"Fayerling," he whispered almost inaudibly, "do you know who Bernard Jenin is?"

"A common thief," replied the baron contemptuously.

"Don't call him that!" snarled the other, with sudden vehemence. "A common thief! And what are we, then?"

"Well, who is the creature, then?"

"It is Sergius!"

The baron started. The news fell upon him like a bolt from the blue, and he stared at Tassler with a look of keen inquiry. Finally he gave a short and somewhat ironical laugh, and said:

"Sergius! The much-talked-of Sergius, whom I have never seen! Of course! Now we know what took him out to the Copper House. I might have guessed."

He reached for the photograph, and examined it carefully, after which he put it back in his pocket.

"So little Sergius has a finger in the pie—on his own account! This will amuse Ortiz immensely. What a joke! Now we have only to hold out our hands for Tarraschin's memorandum: Sergius will be delighted to give it up to you as soon as he sees you, Tassler."

"He loathes me."

"That's no business of mine, it's your own affair. All I can say is that you must manage to get speech with him, by Lona Ivanovna's help. Why man, with such cards in our hands, we can't help winning the game. When is the next train to Karkby?"

Tassler's fishy eyes seemed to conceal all manner of dark and crafty thoughts.

"When is the Chief to arrive?" he asked after a pause.

"This evening, or, at latest, tomorrow."

"How much does he know?"

"Nothing of Sergius' arrival, or Wallion's interference. He expects to find Tarraschin's memorandum in our hands; his plans are ripe, and he is growing impatient. Things are going to move a bit in the Copper House, before we are many hours older. Every man is at his post, and we mustn't let any risks hinder us now. Come along."

He took Marcus Tassler by the arm, and they went out together.

As soon as breakfast was over, Leo hurried up to his room, but Maurice Wallion was no longer there. A little thread of blue smoke was still curling up from a cigarette in an ash-tray on the window-ledge; the window had been fastened, which Leo interpreted to mean that the Problem-hunter had not left the room that way, but was making a reconnaissance inside the house.

The young man went out into the corridor, and before he could say "Jack Robinson" the journalist confronted him, calm and smiling. Leo started, and looked anxiously round, but Wallion said:

"Go downstairs again, and try not to look as though you were accessory to a crime! I have only been looking about me a little. Where does that winding staircase lead to, in the lumber-room at the back?"

"Down to a little passage between the kitchen and the back door," replied Leo.

"Can one reach the first floor that way?"

"Yes, there is a landing and a door there."

"That's fine! Have you met Andrei Bernin?"

Leo described in a few words what had taken place.

Wallion smiled again, and said:

"So they are expecting me?"

"Yes, anxiously. Something seems to have alarmed them; they have quite changed their attitude since yesterday."

The Problem-hunter nodded thoughtfully.

"That's to be expected; they are beginning to wake up now. I shall set to work when Marcus Tassler has been here."

"Do you think he is coming?"

"Yes, he is bound to. You must receive him!"

Wallion fixed his gray eyes for a moment on Leo.

"You are keeping cool, that is right. Don't forget that I am here."

He nodded once more, and slipped quietly away. Leo saw him vanish in the direction of the back stairs; he was beginning to think that this man was independent of sleep at night, and breakfast in the morning, and he marveled at the buoyancy of his disposition.

Sonia Bernin's voice called from below:

"Mr. Grath, where are you?" and he went downstairs.

A bank of cloud was drifting slowly up from the direction of Stockholm; the sun shone palely from an almost colorless sky. A distant rumble of thunder sounded through the uncomfortably close atmosphere like the echo of a cannonade.

The young man went out with the girl into the garden. He could see, through the dining-room window, the blind man sitting in the shadow of the curtain, with his sister, who was working as usual. At some distance away in the garden, a man with a knife was cutting a bunch of red flowers. He wore a broad-brimmed straw hat, and a blue apron. It struck Leo that the garden was the only part of his property that showed signs of being carefully, and even lovingly tended. It was fragrant with the scent of old-fashioned flowers: silky-soft sweet peas, white stocks, and modest mignonette, growing between beautiful crimson and deep yellow roses. A carpet of velvety pansies contrasted with the brilliant display of sunflowers, peonies and dahlias. Some way off, the orderly ranks of the useful vegetables were marshaled; pale-green, dark-green, and purple cabbages, crimson beetroots, and regular masses of radishes, carrots and parsley. Cucumbers lay beneath the panes of the forcing-frames, and behind the glass walls of the hothouses was a mighty though nondescript array of reserve forces in green uniforms.

"What colors!" said Leo. "Your gardener must be an artist...."

"That's Rosenthal," said the girl, pointing towards the man in the blue apron. "He is mad on flowers!"

They approached the man, who looked up as they reached him. His face was fair but sunburnt, with light-blue eyes and a kindly mouth. He touched his cap, but in such a way that Leo saw at once that he was a well-bred man.

"Good morning," said Leo: "'il faut cultiver notre jardin,' n'est-ce-pas?"

"Voltaire was wrong there," replied the man quietly: "it is not a duty, but a pleasure to cultivate a garden."

He spoke as to an equal, and Leo raised his eyebrows and looked at him more attentively. There was something military in his bearing, but his speech was that of an educated man, and his thoughtful eyes were those of a poet.

"You love color, don't you?" Leo continued.

"Yes," answered the man, "especially purple; it is the color of royalty—and of revolution."

"A good idea," Leo agreed. At that minute he felt the girl give his arm a little tug.

The man went on quietly with his flower-cutting, and after a second's almost awkward silence, Leo turned away, feeling that he had been tacitly dismissed.

"Why did you pull my arm?" he asked, softly.

"It is Rosenthal," whispered the girl: "he speaks in a way that somehow frightens me. And Rastakov too...." Sonia's voice broke a little; her complexion looked transparently clear this morning.

"Everything seems so strange since last night," she went on: "something is going to happen!"

"What is it? Why won't you be frank with me?"

The girl did not reply. They were standing amongst the rose-bushes at the corner of the terrace. Some distance away in the garden, Rosenthal straightened himself up, shading his eyes with his hand. As he looked down the avenue a whistle sounded suddenly from the direction of the gate; he threw down his knife, and went off to the kitchen, carrying the cut flowers in his apron. He came out again almost immediately, and walked quickly away. At the same time, Lona Ivanovna opened the front door, and stepped out on to the terrace.

Two persons now appeared in the avenue: one was Rastakov, the other a short, stout gentleman, who looked very warm and agitated.

"Do you know who that is?" whispered Sonia.

"No," answered Leo.

"It is Marcus Tassler."

The newcomers went up to the terrace, where Lona Ivanovna received them with what seemed to Leo to be an air of undisguised hostility.

"You come in good company, Marcus! But, to make your trio quite complete, you should have brought the baron with you. What do you want?"

Tassler went up to her; his eyes were bloodshot, and his face had turned a sort of sickly gray color.

"Baron Fayerling is here," he answered hoarsely, "he is coming immediately; where is Sergius?"

"And *you* ask for Sergius?" she exclaimed shrilly. "You have no right—"

"Who has a better right than I?"

"You have forfeited it. Besides, things have changed; I don't trust you any longer, Marcus. Mind what you are about! The fire is kindled, opposition awaits you at every turn—and as for Sergius, he is where you will never get hold of him!"

"Lona Ivanovna," said Tassler in a stifled voice: "I warn you, it is impossible to stop us!"

Sonia had seized Leo's hand quite unconsciously in hers and was squeezing it tightly.

"Oh, God! Oh, God!" she moaned softly.

Tassler turned his head and caught sight of them. Leo went up to him, and both men raised their hats simultaneously, whilst the young man said:

"I am pleased to meet you, Mr. Tassler; I am Leonard Grath. I don't know if you have come out here to see me, but in any case...."

"Yes, I have come to speak to you," said the other heavily. "I hear that you no longer wish to sell the Copper House: is that true?"

"Perfectly true," replied Leo politely.

Marcus Tassler looked at him as though this reply was not unexpected, and puffed away at his cigar.

"My client is prepared to increase his offer," he said after a minute.

Leo smiled.

"It is not a question of increasing the offer, but of the entire rejection of any offer whatsoever.... Besides, your client is Mr. Andrei Bernin, isn't he? I have been talking to him, but he didn't allude to the matter; it does not seem to interest him any longer," added the young man boldly. Lona Ivanovna stood listening to them, her eyes bright, and her lips tightly shut: but she said nothing. Tassler turned to her:

"Can I see Andrei Ivanovitch?" he asked sharply; "Rastakov tells me that your brother is up...."

The old lady turned, and went indoors.

"Allow me to show you the way, gentlemen," she said, over her shoulder. Her voice and look bore traces of an inward conflict.

Another peal of thunder rumbled in the distance.

CHAPTER X

The Situation Becomes Acute

Maurice Wallion had gone down the winding staircase just as the gardener came into the kitchen, and from his hiding place he heard Rosenthal inquire in a low voice:

"Where is Rastakov?"

A gruff voice, which obviously belonged to the man on guard by the kitchen door, replied:

"He is at the lodge."

There was a little rustling sound, as Rosenthal threw the roses down on a table, and he called out:

"Here are your roses, Lona Ivanovna. I hear you have visitors, and Tassler and the baron are expected," and without waiting for an answer, the gardener went out again. Wallion, who had remained motionless on the stairs, heard a distant sound from the front of the house, and hesitated over his next move. Presently he went up to the first floor and, after listening a little, he opened a window at the back of the house, and jumped softly down. He slipped into the shrubbery, and skirted the wall of the terrace until he came in sight of the main entrance. He heard the old lady request the gentlemen to follow her, and saw them enter the house behind her. Rastakov and the young girl remained together, and the former said shortly:

"What are you waiting for?"

She went up to him, and said, in a grave voice that contrasted oddly with her girlish appearance:

"Justice must be done. That is what I am waiting for." She looked straight at Rastakov's swarthy face, and he returned her gaze fixedly.

"Justice! That is a wonderful word, Sonia Andreievna. There is no justice nowadays; the bayonets have put an end to it. The future is blood-red, Sonia Andreievna; don't pin your hopes to it."

He spoke in a hard, bitter voice, then turned and left her.

The girl put both her hands up to her face, and ran down the terrace; like some little lost animal, she stood still, then ran on again, crying softly to herself. At last she threw herself on to a bench, under the shade of the syringa trees, crouched down in the farthest corner of it, and buried her face in her arms. A low murmur of voices could be heard through the open windows of the dining-room.

Wallion, concealed by the trees, took a few steps towards the avenue, and saw in the distance Baron Fayerling approaching, accompanied by the lodge-keeper, Tugan, and two of the forest-guards. They were walking briskly along, at the pace of a marching patrol. At the same moment, the Problem-hunter made another, and far from reassuring discovery: across the field on either side of the avenue, he noticed a number of men, posted at equal distances from each other, and stretching as far as the eye could reach…a double "cordon" was being drawn round the Copper House. Double, indeed: for when Wallion turned round, he saw five or six fellows with guns file on to the terrace from the opposite direction, and take up their position close to the house. No chance of getting past them!

He was caught in a trap: the outer "cordon," which embraced a considerable area, was being gradually contracted. He calculated the number of men to be about forty.

"They have brought reinforcements," he reflected. "Something must be going to happen; the gang is assembling—they only want the great, invisible Gabriel Ortiz to make things complete"; and he looked all round him, and bit his lips. A few raindrops were beginning to patter on the dry leaves, and towards the sea, dark thunder-clouds were gathering in heavy masses.

* * * *

Lona Ivanovna appeared again; she went over to her niece and took her by the shoulder.

"Come indoors," she said softly and gently; "Sonia, I believe that a miracle *might* happen, but we must keep a brave face, and never cry for quarter."

The girl got up; her eyes were dry now, and she took her aunt's hand, like a child, and went in with her.

It was very quiet in the dining-room, where the others were assembled. Tassler was standing in the middle of the room, Leo by the window on the right-hand side, and Rastakov—his arms theatrically folded—by the door. No one was speaking, but it was evident that something had just been said which astonished them, and they were all looking at the blind man in his armchair, as though they expected him to say something more.

Andrei Bernin was sitting with his white head turned towards them: now and then, he rubbed his hands as though they were cold, but he remained silent.

"It is very strange," said Tassler at length, in a thick, grumbling voice: "it is most extraordinary, Andrei Bernin, that you did not find this out before. You state that you no longer wish to buy the Copper House, because you are too poor! You owe both Mr. Grath and myself an explanation."

"I never said that I was rich enough to buy the Copper House: it is as much as I can afford to remain here as its tenant. Why do you ask me, Marcus, when you know that you have always managed everything?"

"Exactly, I undertook to see to all your business for you. You—poor? Why, man, you have been ill for so long, that your ideas have grown quite hazy! Your money has multiplied enormously, invested in the Finno-Russian Import and Export Company: don't you realize that?"

Tassler spoke rapidly and loudly, as though he anticipated some interruption; he mopped his cheeks and forehead with his handkerchief, and looked at Andrei Bernin with a very unwonted expression of obsequious servility.

"Surely you are capable of understanding as much of your business as that," he continued…"of course, I have done my best for you."

"Perhaps," answered the blind man; "perhaps you have, Marcus; but I am not going to buy the Copper House."

Tassler lifted his small, plump hands, and turned to Lona Ivanovna.

"Always the same! This poor brother of yours hasn't the slightest idea of business! I begin to think that you must have acted on your own responsibility during his illness. Can't you make him see reason?"

"I don't think that is necessary," she answered quietly.

"You don't?"

"No, not since yesterday—when Sergius came here."

"Sergius!"

"Yes—Marcus, up to yesterday, I still believed in you, and allowed you to act for us. That's all over. Now you must act for yourself."

"And that is the most difficult of all," added the feeble voice of the blind man, philosophically.

Marcus Tassler turned distinctly paler; it was impossible to ignore the challenge in Lona Ivanovna's tone and whole demeanor. Even Leo noticed it, and to relieve the painful tension, he said pleasantly, and as unconcernedly as he could:

"Yes, there we are agreed, my dear Mr. Tassler. When the purchaser will not buy, nor the seller sell, the whole transaction comes automatically to an end. For the exact details, I must ask you to be so good as to refer to Mr. Burchardt."

Tassler turned to him, with the ponderous agility of a hippopotamus.

"I will do so, Mr. Grath."

"That will be all right, then."

"And I shall tell him that you have refused the best offer that has ever been made for a property," continued Tassler. "*My* conscience is clear, at any rate."

"Not altogether, Marcus," said the blind man from his corner.

Tassler's obsequiousness cracked like a mirror at a blow from a hammer, and behind the mirror appeared a very different face, with angry eyes, distorted features, and lips drawn back in an ugly snarl.

"Listen to me, Andrei," he cried out quickly and breathlessly: "and you too, Lona. I can see quite well that Sergius has bewitched you. Take care! Sergius is not what he was, he has taken the wrong road, and anyone who shelters him is bound to be ruined."

"What do you want?" she asked.

"I want to speak to him, before it is too late."

"It is *too* late, now!"

"That's impossible!"

"Marcus Tassler, it is all over. You cannot alter things now."

"Not I, perhaps, but certainly…."

"Certainly who?" a voice interrupted him, and the baron came into the room. "Can you mean me, by any chance?"

Tassler was silent. The baron had staged his entrance with the skill and aplomb of an accomplished actor. He advanced with the friendly air of a casual visitor, but no one could ignore the imperious gesture with which he imposed silence upon his partner. The lash was inflicted with a smile:

"By Jove, Tassler, how you do hold forth! Madame Ivanovna, don't let us dispute over trifles. Be so good as to introduce me to your brother and to the owner of the Copper House."

As the old lady did not move, he completed the ceremony himself, with easy grace, pressing the blind man's passive hand, and bowing low to Leo.

"You have a remarkably fine old property, Mr. Grath," he remarked, "but it is very much out of the world, and all sorts of strange things might happen here, without anybody having the slightest suspicion of what was going on. I am thinking more particularly of the case of Bernard Jenin, and what is likely to be the result of it."

He smoothed his D'Annunzio beard, looked from one face to another, and repeated thoughtfully:

"What the results may be."

A pause followed these words. The blind man remarked:

"Logic teaches us that one of two results will follow: either Bernard Jenin will be captured, or he will not. I incline towards the latter hypothesis."

"Indeed!" replied the baron. "Logic is a wonderful science, my dear Mr. Bernin; I also argue logically, and I say: Bernard Jenin certainly came to the Copper House; he certainly did not leave it again: therefore he must still be in the Copper House. It is as easy to prove as this other little syllogism: Thieves deserve punishment: Bernard Jenin is a thief: therefore Bernard Jenin deserves punishment."

"Are you not first bound to prove that he is a thief?" suggested Leo, and Sonia flashed a grateful look at him.

The baron affected to be much surprised, and turned courteously to the speaker:

"Certainly," he admitted, "but only to those whose business it is to plead for the thief."

Leo colored.

"As the owner of the Copper House," he said more sharply, "it seems to me that I have a right to know whether I am harboring a thief in my house, or not."

"Most assuredly. Will it content you if I can show that the fellow robbed me?"

Leo replied with a stiff bow.

"Well, Mr. Grath, allow me to inform you that an important paper—the so-called Tarraschin memorandum—whilst on its way to me from Russia, was stolen by Bernard Jenin, and is still in his possession. Tassler and Rastakov are my witnesses; is that sufficient?"

"Yes, if no one takes exception to your statement, or to your witnesses." Leo looked at Lona Ivanovna, but, to his surprise, she turned her face away.

The baron smiled superciliously, and the young man, irritated, he knew not why, said deliberately:

"No doubt you are right; and you are quite at liberty to call in the police."

Rastakov made an involuntary movement, but the baron checked him with a glance, and answered:

"The police? Yes, I would do so, if I had plenty of time to spare, and if I was not unwilling to compromise my dear friends here—" and he looked at Andrei Bernin and the two ladies. "As it is essential that I should have the paper by this evening, I must unfortunately take the matter into my own hands."

"Leave him alone!" interrupted Lona Ivanovna harshly, turning to Leo: "haven't you had enough of his accursed conversation?"

Rastakov, Tassler and the baron burst out laughing.

"You are really *too* delightful, Madame!" said the last named person; "what do you say, Mr. Grath? Have we your leave to search for Bernard Jenin?"

"I am of the same opinion as Madame Bernin," replied the young man, with equivocal civility.

Baron Fayerling's smile vanished.

"Then we quite understand one another, Mr. Grath?"

"Perfectly, baron."

The baron stepped out through the open window, and shouted a few words in Russian. A dozen figures hurried up from the terrace, and marched noisily into the hall. The baron exchanged a couple of sentences with Tassler, in a rapid undertone, and went out into the hall with Rastakov.

Marcus Tassler sat heavily down on a chair, and stared at Lona Ivanovna, who, with unruffled composure, had returned to her place near her brother; she went on with her crochet and took no notice of Tassler.

"What a cold-blooded woman you are, Lona," said the merchant, in a rather faltering voice. "After all, this affects Sergius...."

"No need to tell me that," she replied, shrugging her shoulders; "you may go to your lord and master: you have nothing to do with Sergius."

He was silenced by the caustic bitterness of her voice, and remained with his mouth open, staring vaguely and irresolutely across the room at the blind man and his sister.

Sonia went quietly up to her father, and leaned her head against his shoulder; the blind man began to stroke her black hair clumsily.

Leo felt acutely distressed: these three unfortunate beings, whom he already regarded as his friends, seemed so far from him, that he could not summon up courage to say another word to them. They were withdrawn into the intimacy of their home-circle, and he remained outside like a stranger. With the agonizing sensation of being the witness of a tragedy into whose inner meaning he had no right to intrude, he left the room silently, without looking at them again.

As he came into the hall, which was empty, a new and alarming thought struck him; what had become of Wallion? He heard the baron's voice, echoing sharp and clear down the well of the staircase.

"Take each floor in turn, and keep guard whilst you search the rooms. You, over there, don't pass over that corner—don't leave a stone unturned. Rastakov, take a couple of men with you, and search the attics thoroughly. Be sharp, now!"

It was evident that the searchers meant to leave nothing to chance this time; the furniture was moved about, the walls sounded, and the tramp of many feet was heard in each room in turn, till the whole house seemed full of men. If there were really anyone hidden in the Copper House, thought Leo, he would certainly be found within ten minutes: what was the journalist doing?

The young man listened, his heart beating fast. Now they were on the second floor, and coming to his room. He ran upstairs, with the desperate intention of preventing them from entering, but he was too late. As he came into the corridor, Rastakov was just leaving the room, and Leo saw with indescribable relief, that the Russian's face was dark with disappointment. They passed one another without a word, and Leo shut himself quickly in.

He flung himself into a chair, and buried his head in his hands; what should he do? His mind refused to work, and he stamped his foot in impotent vexation.

Had the journalist been caught in a trap, and helplessly resigned himself to his fate? Had he discovered Bernard Jenin's hiding-place?

"Did you look in here?" he heard the baron ask just outside the door.

"Yes," answered another voice further along the passage; "Rastakov has been there."

"Go on, then."

The steps and voices grew fainter. Leo had not raised his head. Suddenly he heard a slight sound on the floor close to his feet; a paper lay there, wrapped round a pebble. He picked it up, and saw that there was something written on the paper; he unfolded it, and read:

"Don't worry, things are going as I expected. I have concluded some useful investigations, and shall soon make myself known. M. W."

Leo sprang up. The window, which had been closed earlier in the day, had been opened later, and he realized that the little note had been thrown in through it. But he could not see a sign of the journalist outside. Only Rosenthal was walking slowly along, in his blue apron and broad-brimmed straw hat.

CHAPTER XI

Maurice Wallion Looks About Him a Bit and Makes a New Acquaintance

As soon as the Problem-hunter saw Baron Fayerling go into the Copper House, he felt convinced that a crisis was at hand.

"Fayerling's arrival is a bad sign," he thought, "I would rather see Ortiz himself. Where on earth can he have got to?"

He lay still for several minutes, wondering how he could manage to dodge the cordon of men which was closing in round him from the direction of the field.

"It's high time I gave Robert Lang his final instructions—but how am I going to do it?" he pondered. "It is important for me to remain here, especially on Grath's account, as it is largely through me that he has got into this fix. The Copper House is completely surrounded, and these fellows would be able to shoot the lot of us, without anyone being near enough to help us. It is odd that they should have left the telephone at the lodge in working order, and cut off the one at the house. If only I could get down to the lodge!"

He took stock of the advancing forces, and made a wry face: as things were, he was obliged to admit that it was impossible to get past them. The only chance of escape was on the other side, towards the sea. He might possibly be able to reach the railway station in some roundabout way, and telegraph or telephone to Lang from there. He crept back along the terrace-wall, almost within reach of the seven or eight men who kept guard above, and began with great circumspection to make his way seawards. He passed behind the stable and cowhouse without meeting anybody, and as soon as he got in amongst the trees at the foot of the ridge, he started running over the soft carpet of brown pine-needles, and short grass. But in a few minutes, hearing steps and voices ahead of him, he turned off to the right. He got an occasional glimpse of the sea, gleaming through the trees, and went on boldly in that direction.

Suddenly he shrank back, and crouched down behind a thick cluster of bracken. Just where the ridge ended, on the left, he had seen three forest-guards walking towards him, and further on his right, between him and the sea, he espied yet another figure with a gun.

Had he been seen? Apparently not, but he decided that with so many men about, that way was impassable, too.

He gazed longingly at the calm, glittering Bay, which was practically an inland sea, the entrance being almost closed by a long, wooded island. Exactly below him, a path ran from the house to a dilapidated pier, on the left of which stood an even more tumble-down marine store, or fisherman's cottage, with a tiled roof and one small, unglazed window. A little way out from the pier was anchored a lighter, of the type of those which one frequently sees being towed in long lines through the island channels. A slender column of smoke was rising from the cabin chimney, and on the gunwale sat a man in a cotton shirt, fishing. While Wallion was watching him, he cautiously drew in his line, and landed a fish, which gleamed like silver in the sunlight.

But it was not the sight of the lonely fisherman which specially attracted the journalist's attention: it was a long, white scar in the side of the lighter, just above the water-line. It looked just as though someone had taken a huge knife and made a gash three or four yards long through the tarred planks. An ice-floe, swept along in a strong current, might have done it—but the mark was fresh, and last winter's ice had melted long ago, under the summer sun.

Wallion roused himself from his speculations, for the men who were descending the ridge were getting dangerously near him, and he beat a retreat for the second time towards the house. He moved without hurry or nervousness, but he was forced to admit that he had never been in a tighter corner, and he felt certain that the men who now surrounded the house had come to stay. It was worthy of notice that these extra guards were drawn up facing the building: evidently their aim was not so much to keep out any unauthorized visitor, as to prevent those inside the house from getting into communication with the outer world. Perhaps they already knew that Wallion was somewhere on the premises! This possibility made him look serious: if they knew where he was to be found, all was up with him. He stood still and listened. The three men were slowly walking along behind him; on the right he could hear other unwelcome sounds of twigs snapping and bushes rustling; there was open ground to the left, but even that was not unoccupied—four of the forest-guards were marching across the field in a line with his hiding place, and if he remained there, nothing could prevent his being discovered.

"What a nuisance," he thought, with annoyance, "I have only one resource left, and that is Rosenthal."

Once more he retraced his steps, passed the cowhouse again, this time on the other side, and scrambled over the palings into the orchard, which at this lower end was neglected, and overgrown with tall, waving grasses.

He now found himself just behind the gardener's little red cottage, and as he peeped cautiously round the corner, he could see one side of the terrace, and the southern wing of the house, with the kitchen door. He saw something else as well: that there was no chance of getting in there now, for men were turning up on all sides, under the windows and behind the bushes; something was going on indoors, probably a fresh search for Bernard Jenin and the memorandum, but no voices could be heard: an almost uncanny silence prevailed.

Wallion kept close to the cottage wall, and stood on tiptoe to look through one of the two windows. The gardener's house consisted apparently of a living-room and a kitchen, with an adjoining tool-house: it was at the window of the latter that he was standing. Nobody was there: the sun shone on hoes, spades, rakes and watering cans, shelves filled with flower pots of all sizes, worn-out scythes, and a perfect arsenal of gardening-knives.

Wallion opened the window with his penknife, and climbed in. Through a door which stood ajar, he could see part of a room alongside: a table by the window, with flowers growing in glasses and pots, a smaller table with books and newspapers on it, and an old rocking-chair.

And in the rocking-chair sat Rosenthal, who called out, as he caught sight of him:

"Good afternoon, Mr. Wallion; I was just expecting you!"

The journalist stepped into the room.

"Did you know that I was in this part of the world?"

"I have seen you already this morning; you are every bit as venturesome as I hoped you would be. I saw you as you were climbing in through the window with Grath. You see, that happened to be my 'beat'; no one has come to or from the Copper House since yesterday afternoon without my knowledge. To avoid all misunderstanding, I may tell you that I also observed our friend Grath's little escapade last evening."

The gardener spoke very deliberately and accurately, with a slight accent. His ruddy face and blue eyes were lighted up with pleasant anticipation. The journalist sat down opposite, and lighted a cigarette, first offering his case, which the other declined. They looked at one another with an expression of mutual understanding.

"You are far more daring than I," said Wallion, "since you have ventured to live in this neighborhood for several months, Mr. Max Raebel."

The gardener got up, and shook Wallion warmly by the hand, then sat down again, smiling all over his face.

"Quite right, I am Max Raebel," he said; "how do you know that, as you have never seen me before?"

"I saw you when you were cutting roses in the garden; in talking to Grath, you raised your head, and I recognized the best detective in Austria, disguised as a gardener. Oh, no need to be modest about it—of course I have heard of you a hundred times, and equally of course, I have your portrait in my collection. I have long suspected that someone of your calibre was taking a hand in the game, but couldn't find out under what name that somebody was working. Since you have managed to secure such a good place—right in the stalls!—I suppose you have succeeded in gaining Fayerling's confidence in some extraordinary way?"

"Not at all, it was perfectly easy; I got a recommendation from Madame Sumensov in Petrograd."

"From Madame herself?"

"Yes, for nobody knows as yet that she serves two masters with equal fidelity!"

"No, it is news to me. You probably know, as I do, that she is a tool of Ortiz? Are you not afraid she may betray you to him?"

"That's one possibility. Another is that I shall have finished my work here before she can do so," replied the Austrian very calmly.

He glanced out of the window.

"They are beginning to get nervous," he added; "nervousness is the beginning of panic, and panic is half-way to defeat."

They both looked at the Copper House for a minute, and saw Rastakov appear at one of the upper windows, and shout an order to the men on the terrace. The baron came out, and looked up at him. Rastakov made an angry gesture, implying that he had had no luck, to which the baron replied with a shrug of his shoulders, and called out in his cool, clear voice: "Look more carefully!"

The Austrian laughed.

"Yes, look, my boy, look!" he echoed.

Wallion turned round.

"In the meantime, Ortiz is on his way here," he remarked.

"Yes," said the other, "we are all waiting for him, aren't we?"

Wallion pulled out his notebook and laid it on the table.

"Mr. Max Raebel, let us compare notes: first, you have only been here since April 29th, at all events under the name of Rosenthal. You only began to interest yourself in Ortiz's affairs after the Tarraschin document appeared on the scene; therefore this document is what you are on the lookout for: may I ask why?"

The Austrian's fair face and friendly eyes clouded over a little, and he did not answer immediately.

"I am no politician," he said finally; "I am a detective, and sent out with a definite end in view. My task is to make sure that Tarraschin's memorandum does not fall among thieves, to prevent it from being illegally employed, and, in the last resort, to destroy it. One of the statesmen of my country, whose name you may perhaps guess, but I must not mention, would be deeply compromised were that document to be unscrupulously handled."

The Austrian bent forward.

"And not only he, but a more exalted personage still," he added.

Wallion opened his eyes.

"Aha," he said, "that is worse than I feared!" He considered a little. "I took it for granted that Tarraschin's scheme affected Russia only."

The Austrian shook his head.

"Let me tell you something, Mr. Wallion; everything that happens nowadays is of world-wide importance; all that concerns Tarraschin's memorandum is highly characteristic of the circumstances which have produced it. Look back a bit; the Russian Revolution had long been expected, but who could have foretold that it would break out in March, 1917? It fell upon Europe like an avalanche, the sudden upheaval of a mighty mass; and not as the immediate result of some great ideal, or political disturbance, but apparently in consequence of the scarcity of food at Petrograd. At all events, the way was prepared for it, and once set going, the landslide crashed down into the depths, leaving devastation in its wake. Was it possible to restore order? This was a question in which all countries were interested. Before anything else, it was of the utmost importance to ascertain the policy of the Russian Conservative party, the State officials, the officers of the army, and certain members of the Tsar's immediate 'entourage'—all those, in a word, who belonged to the governing class. Would they be strong enough to organize a counter-revolution before the new men had grown powerful enough to check them? Even on March 15th, the Tsar had virtually abdicated the throne; was that a sign of the disintegration and consequent ineffectiveness of the reactionary party? No, for they still had a symbol round which to rally: there was the army. At that moment, Prince Tarraschin appeared on the scene. Do you know his history?"

"Yes, more or less. He was one of the most typical leaders of the old régime. It was he who got the reputation of having run through one fortune every year! He was a daring politician, and a friend of the Grand Duke Nicolai—an intelligent man, and perhaps an honorable one, according to his lights."

"There is no doubt as to his intelligence," said the Austrian; "now let me tell you what he did. One can hardly say that the Revolution ruined him, for he had just about ruined himself. But he could not bring himself to accept it: to him, the Revolution was the end of all things. His one idea was that power and mastery must be regained at any cost. He set to work undauntedly, and for a short time it looked as though he would succeed in winning over the strongest element in the Conservative party to his cause. He drew up an ingenious scheme of counter-revolution; he had two methods of dealing with waverers: promises and money. The history of Tarraschin's promises you have probably never heard: it is like a fairy tale."

"Go on, go on," said Wallion, as the Austrian stopped; "I know something about Tarraschin's correspondence with certain individuals in Austria."

Max Raebel raised his eyebrows.

"You know that, do you? But you say 'certain individuals,' there was only one, the Austrian statesman to whom I alluded just now. The highly confidential correspondence between him and Tarraschin had to do with Balkan affairs and was concluded before the outbreak of the March Revolution. There was no question, as people declared, of any understanding with Austria, in the event of the establishment of a democratic Russian monarchy desirous of peace; it was an absolutely private discussion between two political specialists, so to speak; yet at this crisis, Tarraschin did not hesitate to avail himself of this correspondence. He represented my countryman's statements in the light of promises inspired by a higher authority, an authority which had, as the whole world knew, an intense desire for peace. In this way, Tarraschin managed to secure one more means of support, calculated to strengthen the weaker brethren amongst the reactionaries. It mattered nothing to him that he was compromising two of the most highly-placed dignitaries in my country. Next, as regards funds—"

"Ah, there our paths meet, Mr. Raebel," broke in Wallion; "the funds for Tarraschin's intended revolution were supplied by Gabriel Ortiz."

"Exactly. Ortiz financed the enterprise through a channel, at one end of which we find Tassler and Fayerling, but at the other, Madame Sumensov and Tarraschin. How much gold has been distributed by their means, is more than I can say."

"I can give you a rough estimate: it was, in round numbers, fifteen to twenty million roubles."

The Austrian laughed.

"Really! A perfect fortune, and the last which Tarraschin had the pleasure of squandering, for, as you know, he died suddenly on the 29th of March. There is no doubt that he was assassinated, and not by the revolutionaries, but by his own friends."

For the first time during their conversation the journalist looked surprised.

"Do you mean his political associates?" he asked.

"Yes. They were mortally afraid, as soon as they realized how irretrievably Tarraschin was about to compromise them. Instead of replacing the crown on the Tsar's head, they were in danger of finding their own heads removed from their shoulders. And with characteristic Russian philosophy they said to themselves: 'It is better that one man die for the people.'... Nevertheless, our friend Tarraschin had already done his worst: he had drawn up a detailed memorandum of the plans for the counter-revolution, in which he had set down with the most scrupulous exactitude what each one of the participators had pledged himself to do—with name, place and time, in full; everything very skilfully thought out, and perfectly feasible, and from a military point of view, quite certain to result in over a hundred executions. And, in addition, as I said just now, it compromised two persons who, like Cæsar's wife, must be above suspicion."

"One might fancy," remarked the journalist, "that Ortiz had had a hand in the production."

"Not a doubt of it: he would want some hold over the men who were receiving his money, and with this paper in his possession he can compel them to do anything he likes. Tarraschin's death is of no consequence in comparison with the possibilities raised by his memorandum. It constitutes the keystone of Ortiz's gigantic scheme: without the memorandum, the whole of his plan will melt into thin air."

"And in consequence, we can pretty well guess his present designs," supplied Wallion.

They looked at one another.

"He is magnificent!" said the Austrian.

"But quite mad!" replied Wallion.

A step was heard outside the window, and a shadow fell across the glass. It was Rastakov. The journalist flattened himself against the wall, with a noiseless wriggle of his body. The gardener got slowly up, yawned loudly, and opened the window.

"What do you want, Rastakov?"

The man outside was breathing heavily.

"Why are you not with us, Rosenthal? The baron wants to know if you have seen anyone leave the Copper House; we cannot find Bernard Jenin anywhere."

"I have not seen any unauthorized person leave the house," said the gardener; "why is the baron so persistent? I told you yesterday evening that Bernard Jenin had disappeared, Comrade Rastakov."

"He cannot have disappeared. He must be somewhere on the premises. The baron has decided that the house and its surroundings are to be totally isolated, I can tell you that. All those inside are prisoners, even Grath. Be ready for anything; the Chief is due this evening, and within the next twenty-four hours we shall probably have cleared out of this."

"You may depend upon me," the gardener reassured him.

Rastakov stood for a minute, shifting undecidedly from one foot to another, then took his departure.

The Austrian's face wore a new expression of military decision and firmness.

"Well, they have burnt their boats now!" said he; "and may I be there to see the end of it," he added after a pause.

CHAPTER XII

In Which We Catch a Glimpse of the Shadow of Napoleon the Great

The Problem-hunter and the Austrian detective remained standing together, and watching from behind the curtains a commotion at the house. Some kind of dispute seemed to be taking place there, the cause of which became apparent when they heard Lona Ivanovna's commanding voice exclaiming: "Out you all go!"

Quite a number of men came tumbling out on to the terrace, and the old lady appeared behind them at the kitchen door; she was like a Valkyrie of old, and the men quailed before her as trees bend before a gale.

"Why, goodness me, men, you have your precious master there, haven't you?" said she, pointing one long, bony finger at the baron; "he can tell you that there isn't a spot the size of a farthing in this house, which hasn't been examined. You can all see that Bernard Jenin is not here; ask your Roumanian baron if he can suggest any corner in which a fugitive could still be hidden."

"That will do, madam," said the baron, sourly; "we have not finished yet: we know what we know...."

"Perhaps you don't know what I know, for all that!"

"And what may that be?"

"That you are a worthy leader of the biggest set of blockheads I have ever seen!" answered the old lady, with a loud laugh, as she shut the door again.

Baron Fayerling shrugged his shoulders, and went off with Rastakov; Marcus Tassler hurried after them, and the three men disappeared down the avenue. But they left the house under the close supervision of a cordon of dark, determined, armed men, who, after a few apparently aimless movements in different directions, extended their line in such a way as to include the gardener's cottage within its limits.

The two detectives at the window commented on this fresh turn of events with critical approval, rather as though they had been two spectators in a box at the Opera.

"Rastakov has managed that well," said Wallion, smiling; "now all the approaches to the house are effectively isolated—and we with them."

At that instant, a sharp shower that almost amounted to a squall, swept over the garden, whirling away, like a gray specter, across the woods to the southwest. A deep stillness followed; everything was motionless, and each little leaf shone like glass in the hot, dazzling sunshine. The broad expanse of the steep copper roof, which was green with verdigris, took on a more richly enameled glow, and the very roses in the garden seemed to deepen in color.

"*You* are isolated," said the Austrian after a moment's silence, "but *I* have a certain amount of liberty—don't forget that I am one of them—for the time being."

The journalist laughed.

"What's become of your two under-gardeners?" he asked.

"Rastakov has mobilized them."

"Are they…."

"They are nothing more nor less than—Bolsheviks!"

It was the first time that the word had been mentioned by either of them, and Wallion bent forward.

"Do you know that for certain? I presume you have discovered that Rastakov has dealings with the Bolshevik gang?"

The other nodded.

"It set me thinking," he admitted; "they support Ortiz with extraordinary keenness, though I don't believe he half knows what ideas Rastakov cherishes inside that ugly mug of his. Of the men he has under his orders, half, to my knowledge, are Bolsheviks, that is, they belong to the extremist party which is working to overthrow Kerensky. Ortiz is working for that also, but from another motive.

"The situation is involved, and if Rastakov gets to know the real import of Tarraschin's memorandum, there may be a surprise in store for our friend Ortiz."

"A Bolshevik revolt is in progress at Petrograd at the present time," remarked Wallion, thoughtfully; "all depends upon what Ortiz intends to do. Do you think he is still there?"

"At Petrograd? I did not know he was there at all: I imagined him to be in Finland!" exclaimed the Austrian.

"Yes, at the beginning of this week I could tell, by various signs, that he was in Petrograd. But now that the Tarraschin memorandum has been snatched from under his very nose, he is naturally coming here, and should arrive this evening, at latest."

"Yes, as soon as it is dark enough."

"Does he always come at night?"

"Always, since the end of March."

"I guessed as much," said the journalist, "when I saw how the side of the lighter had been knocked about: some sort of craft had evidently come alongside in the dark. But tell me, why does that blue light, which looks like an acetylene flare, appear every evening?"

"It is some kind of signal which they show from the lighter, and it burns every evening at such times as Ortiz is expected. They do it these nights, especially, as they are engaged in shifting a secret cargo on board the lighter."

"A secret cargo? Arms, you mean?"

"Yes, a good deal of stuff was brought here on the motor-launch *Nelly's* contraband trips. It was a sad blow for Ortiz when the *Nelly* was captured, but, as one would expect, they had obliterated all traces very skilfully, and the police made no search here. There are still several thousand Mauser rifles, packed in wine-cases, as well as a quantity of other articles, calculated to influence Russian opinion as regards the reactionary program!"

Whilst the Austrian talked, he was unconsciously smelling a fragrant, red rose, which he had picked up, and his voice was as unruffled as a mild spring day.

"Where did they store all those things before they were moved to the lighter?" asked Wallion.

"Isn't that down in your notes, yet?" retorted the other, looking up from his rose with a smile.

"I was looking round a bit, and it struck me what a good hiding place there would be under the hay in the cowhouse."

"You've hit it! What sharp eyes you have! But I don't think we need waste much time over contraband goods. Only a minimum of weapons have been despatched from here; Ortiz has probably bought the greater part of his stock in Russia itself, for the ruffians who once formed the Tsar's fine army, sell everything they can lay hands on—rifles, machine-guns, ammunition, everything—even heavy artillery! And to anyone who wants them! And cheap!—eight or ten roubles for a nice little cannon: five for a machine-gun."

The Austrian burst out laughing, and Wallion smiled.

"These are fine times for adventurers," said he; "we need only look out of the window to see that. What an extraordinarily tangled web the War has woven in this one little spot. Bernard Jenin with the Tarraschin memorandum: Baron Fayerling and Marcus Tassler with Ortiz' millions: Rastakov with his Bolsheviks: the Bernin family: the question of contraband: and at the back of them all, the hitherto invisible Gabriel Ortiz, with his shadowy and fantastic schemes."

"If we could get hold of the memorandum, we could break up the whole gang," interrupted the Austrian; "if only I knew what they had done with Jenin!"

"You still think he is in the house?" asked the journalist, with an odd smile.

"Most assuredly, for he has never left it, that I can swear to. You have not once gone in or out unobserved: *I* saw you. Oh, he is certainly there—but where?"

Maurice Wallion wrote a few lines on a piece of paper, and handed it to his companion.

"Will you do me the favor of getting this in some way or other to Leonard Grath?" he said. "I won't show myself yet, though there is little more for us to talk about, except the beginning of all these mysteries. Perhaps you never heard of the Emperor of the Amazons?"

"No," replied the gardener, looking surprised.

"Then I'll tell you about him; I'll wait for you here, whilst you deliver my message to Grath."

The other man looked curiously at him, and said: "Good! I can see you are better informed on some subjects than I am. You stay here, and if you think you hear anyone else coming, just go into the tool-house—you'll be safe there—or go up into the loft."

He indicated a wooden staircase in the corner, took up the note, and went out. Wallion watched him from the window go slowly up the garden, and disappear round the house. Dark faces popped up here and there behind the bushes at the sound of his footsteps, but on seeing that it was Rosenthal, they vanished again noiselessly.

Five minutes later he returned, and Wallion noticed, with some annoyance, that he was now accompanied by two stalwart forest-guards, of a peculiarly bovine cast of countenance.

The three men stopped outside the door, and a lively conversation followed, in which they were joined by five or six of the other men, who came strolling up to listen. Suddenly a name was mentioned which made the journalist prick up his ears.

"Wallion isn't far off," said one of the men.

"And who may he be?" growled another.

"Rastakov says he is a detective. It looks as though we may have to get out of this tonight, if we have a fellow of that sort on our track, but if he turns up before we are ready to quit, I guess he'll find trouble awaiting him. We needn't be too particular now, you know!"

"But how shall we get away from here?" asked a doubtful voice.

"Oh, don't bother me, that's the Chief's look-out: he'll see to that when he comes. What are you going to do, Rosenthal?"

"Go indoors, and get a bit of sleep," replied the gardener. "I was on guard all last night, it's your turn now; besides, we've all got to be up tonight."

A chorus of protest greeted this announcement, but Rosenthal dispersed them with a few vigorous expressions, and, as soon as they were gone, he opened the door, and came in to his visitor.

"Grath has got your note," he said quietly. "I threw it in at his window, and made sure that he had picked it up, before I came away. Did you hear what those fellows were saying?"

"I seem to be in great demand!" replied Wallion.

"They believe that you are on your way here; two men are awaiting your arrival at the station, and others are patrolling the roads. Practically the whole gang is assembled here, and ripe for anything. The baron has shown them your portrait, so they know what you look like, and if you attempt to leave here, and to get into communication with your friends, you had better take the precaution of having an aeroplane handy!"

"I shall certainly stop where I am: it's very cosy here," said Wallion. "But where did the baron get a picture of me?"

"He probably cut it out of some newspaper. What do you say to having a bit of lunch, whilst we discuss the situation?"

"I say yes, with all my heart," laughed the journalist. "Can we count on being left in peace for so long?"

"Yes, on the whole. The baron and Tassler have returned to Stockholm, and are not expected back for three or four hours: this is the calm before the storm."

The Austrian set to work on his preparations for lunch with the skill of an old campaigner, and the journalist lent a hand, so that in a quarter of an hour's time they were sitting down to a simple but plentiful meal.

When they had finished, Wallion lighted a cigarette, leaned back in his chair, and looked at his watch.

"Three o'clock," he remarked. "Let's have a chat, before things get going again."

"Yes," said the Austrian eagerly. "You mentioned a very curious title: 'Emperor of the Amazons,' I think it was; what sort of a Royal Nonesuch was he?"

"You don't know the history of Gabriel Ortiz' earlier fortunes, then?"

"Oh, does it concern him? No, I have never heard his story: it ought to be an interesting one: let's hear it, at all events."

The journalist gave a brief sketch of Ortiz' youthful escapade in Paris, his rash adventure as Emperor of the Amazons, and his daring finance as the "Coffee-King" of Wall Street. The Austrian listened with breathless interest, and as Wallion finished, he exclaimed:

"All this is new to me. One may call it a fit prelude to the great drama of his life. That he imagines himself to be descended from the great Napoleon, explains a good deal; he is not the first to delude himself with that fable, and I daresay that he, like most of the other 'soi-disant' descendants of Napoleon, has altogether omitted to provide any proofs of his statement?"

"He stated that his grandfather was a natural son of Napoleon the Great, born during his captivity at St. Helena; the mother was said to be a young Creole, named Anita Ortiz. To begin with, Gabriel Ortiz' father, at that time a wealthy Brazilian citizen, became acquainted with the great secret of his family, and for many years he sought in vain to establish the facts. After the Amazon adventure, Ortiz was interviewed by an American reporter and was simple enough to boast that, with his noble birth, and his genius, he would show the world once again to what heights a descendant of Napoleon could rise. The result was, that the well-known Professor Hichens devoted twenty minutes of his valuable time to our friend, and within that time, completely annihilated his claim. The Professor proved that no woman named Anita Ortiz had ever been at St. Helena at the time specified, and that all the so-called natural descendants of the imprisoned Emperor had been shown beyond a doubt to be impostors. As far as I know, Gabriel Ortiz had nothing to say in reply. The whole thing was simply the creation of a young man's imagination, but very characteristic of this particular man."

"It is certainly most remarkable," said the Austrian thoughtfully. "I have seen him out here twice, and he really does very strongly resemble the Little Gray Corporal. He is short, pale and clean-shaven, with thin dark hair, which he wears brushed over his forehead, a determined mouth, and dark, gray-blue eyes, expressive of a despotic will and a love of power. One is almost tempted to think…."

Wallion interrupted him:

"Don't let us worry ourselves over it, it doesn't really affect the case: we can allow that Ortiz has a genuine talent for play-acting, can't we? The important thing is to anticipate his wild schemes before it is too late. Everything depends upon who has the Tarraschin document in his possession by the end of today: and to get hold of it, we have only to find Bernard Jenin."

"Which is not going to be so easy as you seem to think!" said the Austrian, rather abruptly. "My dear Mr. Wallion, don't underrate the baron and Rastakov: they are admirable sleuth-hounds, though they have had no luck so far."

"And, therefore," retorted the journalist, "it must be a point of honor with us to beat them at their own game! Don't you yourself insist that Jenin must still be in the Copper House, living or dead? Why, my good sir, the

Copper House isn't like London: a man hidden in it can't remain hidden indefinitely, after all! The sooner we can get speech with him, the sooner we shall be able to control the entire situation. I suggest...."

He paused, frowning a little, then smiled and continued:

"Of course, we must proceed with a certain amount of diplomacy, and whatever happens, we must start with Lona Ivanovna as our ally; I'll see to all that."

"Have you a plan?"

"I have three! But before anything else, you must, on my behalf, get into communication with Robert Lang. You need only say a few words to him, he will know what he has to do. Do you think you can manage it?"

The Austrian nodded.

"Yes, I can telephone at any time from the lodge; in case of need, I have these to back me up," and he pointed with grim satisfaction to his hip-pockets, in each of which reposed a burnished steel "Browning," of the most powerful pattern.

"I can make things pretty hot for them, if the worst comes to the worst," he added; "this is my last resource, and when I use it, it will mean that my own life is at stake. None of us will come out of this alive, if they discover us too soon, but I think we still have a good chance. What am I to tell your friend Lang?"

Wallion considered:

"Tell him that there is no need to get anxious about the baron and Rastakov until they get back here, which they should be allowed to do unmolested, though under surveillance. Also say to him that 'tonight's the night'.... Hallo, what's that?"

He leaned forward and looked out of the window.

"What is that young scatterbrain up to now?"

Leo had come out of the house, accompanied by Sonia Bernin. The young man seemed to have some special object in view, for, as the journalist watched him, he ran quickly across the terrace, followed by the girl.

CHAPTER XIII

Lona Ivanovna asks a Second
Question And Gets An Unexpected Reply

As soon as Leo had read Wallion's message, a feeling of great relief came over him. For the first time he dared to confess to himself that he had been on the point of giving up hope altogether. The realization of Baron Fayerling's true character had brought home to him his own utter helplessness. No one knew better than he that the isolated position of the Copper House gave, for the time being, a tremendous advantage to this dangerous gang; the baron's high-handed proceedings had also made him fear that the journalist—his only friend at this crisis—had already been secretly done away with. But the little slip of paper, so unexpectedly flung through his window, came like a sunbeam into a darkened room: Wallion was evidently still free, and at work. How, under present conditions, he had managed to evade the enemy, was more than Leo could imagine, but the mere knowledge of the fact exhilarated him like a glass of champagne; he drew a deep breath, and his mind, which had seemed frozen, began to work once more. The situation was, after all, full of possibilities as long as Wallion was anywhere in the neighborhood. The wish to do something himself returned to Leo with double force, and one idea after another chased through his active brain; he had a dangerous craving to lend a hand, to surprise his friend by some clever move, some stroke of genius that might even settle the whole affair for good.

He thrust the note into his waistcoat pocket, left his room, and ran whistling downstairs.

In the hall he found Lona Ivanovna, very quiet, and with a look of painfully-concentrated thought on her thin face. He noticed at once that the guard by the door had disappeared, and that quite a new kind of silence reigned over the house; a silence that kept one's ears and nerves perpetually on the stretch. The rooms, whose doors stood open on every side of the hall, gave one the impression of having only just been vacated, and that at any minute something might happen in them.

A flash of lightning flickered from the heavy bank of clouds outside, like the expiring ray of a searchlight, and was followed by a low growl of very distant thunder.

Lona Ivanovna turned, as she heard the young man's step on the stairs.

"They have gone," said she, "and they have not found him yet."

Leo glowed with satisfaction: for the first time the pugnacious old lady addressed him in the friendly tone hitherto reserved for her brother and Sonia. He was quite pleased to hear that Bernard Jenin had not been found, but that was not the most important thing from his point of view.

"Has the baron gone away?" he asked, eagerly.

"Yes, he went just now, with that miserable creature Tassler. But it's too soon to rejoice, my boy, Rastakov is left behind, and we are prisoners," she added in a dry sarcastic tone, as if she found this fact rather amusing.

"Prisoners!" echoed Leo; "how can that be? You must be joking. There is no prison here."

"Dear me, how shall I make you understand!" she muttered, scratching her forehead with her crochet-hook; "have you ever been in the fortress of St. Peter and St. Paul?"

"No, never!" cried Leo, considerably taken aback.

"So I should think. But *I* have! It was in the days when I used to throw bombs," she said confidentially; "well, it would have been easier to escape from Peter and Paul than to get out of the Copper House now. Of course, I was young then...."

Leo stared at her, opened his mouth and—remained silent. He went over to the glass door, threw it open, and hurried out on to the terrace.

"Where are you off to?" demanded Rastakov, appearing in front of him, with his right hand in his pocket.

"Whatever business is it of yours!" retorted Leo furiously. "How dare you speak to me like that! I go where I choose."

Rastakov sneered provokingly.

"Yes, after eleven or twelve o'clock tonight, maybe; but until then you have got to keep quiet, or you may find yourself taken elsewhere first thing in the morning. Go indoors, and get your friends to amuse you; we have a small job on out here, and don't want to be interfered with: so that's all there is to it."

Leo took a couple of steps towards him, but the man quietly drew a huge revolver from his pocket; his face was grim and watchful.

"I mean it!" he said; "go indoors."

Leo looked all round him; he could not repress a shudder as he counted nine or ten armed men posted in front of the house, and he guessed that it would be equally well guarded on the remaining sides; Lona Ivanovna was right: they were prisoners.

"You must be mad!" he exclaimed; "we are not in Russia. I have only to report this to the police, and you would all be arrested."

"Do so, by all means," replied the other scornfully; "perhaps you would like me to send the message for you!"

"I shall—I shall...."

Leo checked himself, and turned back into the house. He was angry with himself, with Rastakov, with the whole world; he was aware that he played a sorry figure, and the knowledge did not improve his temper. However, the recollection of Wallion's message was some consolation, and by the time he saw Lona Ivanovna again in the hall, he was able to speak to her almost cheerfully:

"I must borrow one of those bombs of yours: I have had a dispute with Rastakov, and couldn't find any argument strong enough to convince him."

She stopped working, laid her bony hand on his arm, and said, with a weary little laugh:

"My boy, it is many years since I imagined that I could set the world to rights with a handful of dynamite in a sardine tin: gunpowder, or words, it all comes to the same in the long run."

They entered the drawing-room as she was speaking, and the blind man's feeble voice chimed in:

"Yes, you are right, it doesn't matter: it all ends in noise. Though a bomb is more straightforward, it seems to me," he added thoughtfully, and as if to himself.

This appeared to be a topic they had often discussed before, and Lona Ivanovna immediately joined issue with her brother.

"Not a single bomb that was ever thrown has improved the world in any way. It was the folly of youth that blinded us to the truth, when we were striving so desperately to bring about Russia's freedom. Russia *is* free now, but it is not our bombs that have brought it about."

"Possibly," answered Andrei Bernin, his voice sounding somewhat stronger; "but it is not finished yet. Who knows whether in this very house...."

His sister made a sudden movement, and he was silent.

After a pause he asked:

"Is the young man here?"

"Yes, he is here. Rastakov has just told him that he cannot leave the house.... Would you like to speak to him?"

"I should like to do so," said Andrei Bernin; "let me give you a piece of advice, Mr. Grath: leave this place as soon as you can."

"How can I do that? You heard...."

"Yes, yes, but give them your word that you will say nothing, and they will let you go. It will be better for you."

"He is right," said Lona Ivanovna, softly; "I will tell you the truth: we who are obliged to stop here are expecting nothing less than a catastrophe. I know you want to help us, but what can you do by yourself? You can leave us with a clear conscience."

"But you? What will you do?"

"We? Oh, it will soon be over, we must just have patience."

Before Leo could reply, Sonia sprang up, her eyes wide open, her hands clutching at her throat.

"Patience! I hate that word," she exclaimed. "I will not be patient, I want to see those wretches beaten, who are using Russia's misery as a step-ping-stone for their own fortunes. It is cowardly to be patient, and I won't...."

Her voice broke, and she turned and went quickly out of the room. Her passionate words left the others silent; they scarcely ventured to look at one another, but at last Leo said:

"She is right. What you said was kindly meant and I am grateful, but let me tell you in my turn that I have no intention of leaving here. I am not a pessimist, and I am intensely anxious to see what will happen, especially as the matter concerns my own house."

He waited an instant for their reply, but none was forthcoming. Andrei Bernin sank back among his cushions, and his sister remained standing by the window. Leo bowed, and went out to see what had become of Sonia; she had not gone further than the stairs, where he found her leaning against the banister. She turned her face to him with a dazed expression, and, in her black dress, she looked so small and frail, that the young man seized her little sunburnt hands impulsively, and said:

"Try to be patient a little longer, won't you? Perhaps help is nearer than you think."

"It will have to come pretty quickly, then," she answered in a low voice; "all the same, I am not afraid."

Leo did not know what to say next. A vague masculine sympathy prompted him to try and console her, but he knew instinctively that she would take it amiss. She drew her hands away, and said gravely:

"There is no need for you to trouble yourself about us; we have been un-invited guests in your house, but it won't last much longer; in a short time we shall have gone for good."

"Yes, but look here!" he cried out impetuously; "that is just what I don't want, I ask nothing better than to know more of you, to be one of your best friends; you persist in keeping me at a distance!"

"You mustn't say that!" whispered Sonia, blushing deeply: "You understand something of what we are suffering: a man's life is at stake, and we are bound to keep silence for his sake...."

"Do you mean Sergius?"

"Yes," she answered softly. "He is hidden here, in spite of all their searching; he is my cousin."

This piece of news struck the young man like a flash of lightning.

"Your cousin! Bernard Jenin your cousin! That explains it. Then he must be…."

"Lona Ivanovna's son." Sonia completed the sentence. Leo's hands trembled with excitement. He felt that Wallion ought to know this at once, and he looked round the hall, almost as though he expected the journalist to be somewhere in it.

"Come!" he exclaimed, "come! You ought to have told me that before. We must go straight to him."

"To whom?"

"Maurice Wallion."

The girl gave a little cry.

"Is he here?"

"I don't know. But we must find out where he is."

Leo had no plan, no idea of what he was going to do. It did not occur to him that by acting too precipitately he might spoil everything, he was only conscious of a frantic desire to do something before it was too late, and he rushed off, dragging the girl after him.

They ran like two children through the silent house, and Leo began to call Wallion loudly by name.

"No, no," the girl hushed him; "don't call, they may hear us."

"We must find him! If Bernard Jenin can hide himself, Wallion can do the same."

"No," said she, "your friend couldn't hide himself here, in the way that Sergius has done."

Leo felt that she was speaking the truth. She knew, then, where Jenin was hidden.

"Then it's impossible," he faltered dejectedly; "Wallion can't be here after all."

"No, he certainly isn't inside the Copper House."

Leo began to wonder whether the journalist had abandoned them to their fate, and his eyes grew dim, but he shook off the feeling of hopelessness which was stealing over him, and said quickly:

"He must be somewhere close by."

A few minutes later, they went boldly out by the kitchen door, and took the path to the garden, their intention being to walk right round the house, in defiance of their jailers.

Rastakov was fortunately not to be seen, but four or five of the sentries shouted to them from a distance.

The girl, who was the more level-headed of the two, picked a rose, and arranged it deliberately in the lapel of her coat.

"Look as unconcerned as you can," she whispered. "They oughtn't to mind our taking a breath of fresh air: when they calm down, we will continue our round...."

But at this moment an unforeseen obstacle blocked their way. Rosenthal came striding towards them from the gardener's cottage, and as soon as he was within speaking distance, he called out in a threatening voice:

"Hallo, my young cockerel, what are you doing out here?"

Leo grew white with rage, and replied furiously:

"Mind what you're saying!"

Rosenthal closed with him, and gave him a formidable blow with his fist, on the point of the chin. Leo staggered back, but noticed with surprise that the blow was not so severe in reality as in appearance. And, next minute, he could hardly believe his own ears, when Rosenthal said, almost inaudibly:

"Hit me back, make the hell of a row, it's for your own advantage!"

The man's eyes were on a level with his, and he was aware of an extraordinarily humorous look in them. But, the next instant, the gardener was bellowing at the top of his voice:

"I'll teach you! Ha! You'd hit me back, would you! Come on then!"

He aimed another blow at Leo, who parried it mechanically, and in another moment they were at it, hammer and tongs, making a fearful din, though not before Rosenthal had whispered again:

"Hit me, shout, and make as much noise as you can! You will soon know the reason."

A whole crowd of Rastakov's men collected round them, laughing loudly, and Rastakov himself came hurrying up, looking exceedingly put out. Leo and Rosenthal were pounding one another to the accompaniment of an uninterrupted flow of strong language from the latter.

"What's all this?" Rastakov's voice broke in sharply: "Back to your posts, every one of you! Give it him well, Rosenthal: but you had better leave enough life in the puppy for him to be able to crawl indoors again."

The combatants were separated, and Leo, still giddy with astonishment, stood staring about him for a minute, then turned and reëntered the house without a word.

Sonia joined him with a radiant face.

"That *was* clever of you!" she said with boyish enthusiasm: "I wish you had killed him!"

"Killed him!" stammered the bewildered young man; "Rosenthal— didn't you hear—he said...."

But he found himself quite unable to explain what had happened: he had a general impression of having had a fight with a good-natured giant, who had been pommeling him out of sheer good will. He hurried in to the brother and sister Bernin, and sat down near them, panting. Lona Ivanovna, who was still standing by the window, turned to him and said dryly:

"May I ask the meaning of that comedy, Mr. Grath? I was watching all the time, and neither of you struck a single blow in earnest."

Leo saw with mortification a change in the expression of Sonia's face.

"Weren't you really fighting?" she asked in a disappointed voice. He made a poor attempt at a smile.

"Either Rosenthal or I must be mad," he said frankly: "the man told me to make as much noise as I could."

"Oh-h," said the old lady, slowly: "is *that* it!" Her bright, bird-like eyes shone, and she added softly:

"That being the case, I wonder if your friend Mr. Wallion would be so kind as to come in now...."

"Thanks, with the greatest pleasure," replied the journalist, coming in from the hall. "Your powers of observation do you credit, Madame."

His entrance seemed as though worked by magic: had he fallen from the sky? Even the blind man half rose from his chair.

"At last!" said Leo, from the bottom of his heart, as he made for the journalist and grasped his hand. Wallion looked at him with a smile:

"I hope you haven't quite crippled Rosenthal?" he inquired. "You two knocked one another about splendidly; everybody crowded up to stare at you; and I had only to walk straight in here. I hope soon to be able to present Rosenthal to you, as a useful and trustworthy friend."

"Do you mean to say," said Leo, amazed, "that Rosenthal faked the whole affair in order that you might get into the Copper House unobserved?"

"Yes, we planned it between us on the spur of the moment. What else was there for us to do? What did you think *you* were going to do, single-handed?"

"Why, of course, we meant to go and find you."

"Me?" said Wallion, gravely. "Couldn't you have waited till I was ready? Yes, I know, you had made a discovery, which we will talk about in a minute."

Leo introduced him to the two ladies; Sonia drew back a little after the first greetings, as though to take stock unobtrusively of the tall journalist, whose decided manner and piercing glance evidently impressed her. Lona Ivanovna shook hands heartily with him, and they seemed to understand one another at once: from that time on, they were on terms of the warmest esteem.

"I hope you will forgive me for keeping in the background until now," said Wallion; "there are plenty of sharp eyes round the Copper House, and I don't want Rastakov to take alarm too soon. But there need be no secrets between us henceforward."

He bent down over Andrei Bernin's chair, and took the invalid's hand in his like a doctor.

"Mr. Andrei Bernin," he continued, "your name has interested me immensely since this morning; you need not be afraid of me: don't turn away from me, for I am a friend."

The journalist's keen eyes were very close now to the blue spectacles:

"It is strange that no one but myself has noticed it!"

"What are you talking about?" murmured the blind man, uneasily.

"Of the fact that out of the letters forming the name Andrei Bernin, one can just as easily make the name of Bernard Jenin."

He patted the invalid's hand, and stood up.

"You need not disguise yourself from me, Mr. Bernard Jenin," he added in a low tone; "or may I say Sergius?"

The man in the armchair swept off the blue spectacles, and looked up into Wallion's face:

"Say Sergius!" he replied as quietly.

CHAPTER XIV

The Story of the Bernin Family

The strange scene passed so rapidly, that the fact it conveyed had been accepted by the three spectators before any of them thought of making a move.

"Why, the blind man can see!" was Leo's first thought; and before his still incredulous eyes, the man in the armchair proceeded to divest himself of his venerable white beard and his poetical white locks, revealing a face twenty years younger, in which Leo recognized with something of a shock, the fugitive of the railway carriage and the avenue, the melancholy young man whose lined face was worn with recent illness. The blind Bernin was merely a fiction: under that disguise the hunted Bernard Jenin had been hidden the whole time. The truth dawned upon Leo as though a blind had been suddenly pulled up.

"Don't take off your wig," said Wallion, "and you had better put on the blue spectacles again. Your disguise is perfectly wonderful: I can't understand how you came to have it at hand yesterday evening?"

Lona Ivanovna took up the tale.

"We had better be quite open with our sharp-sighted guest, Sergius. How long has it taken you to see through our poor little stratagem, Mr. Wallion?"

"I suspected something of the kind before I got here," explained Wallion, "otherwise the disappearance of the fugitive would have been nothing short of miraculous. And then the name helped me: how could you be so daring as to call yourself Bernard Jenin, which is neither more nor less than an anagram on Andrei Bernin?"

"That was in case I came to grief," answered the fugitive; "if my mother saw that name in the papers, she would know that it referred to me. Years ago, sitting round the table after the lamp was lighted, we used to amuse ourselves making anagrams on our names. For instance, Sonia Bernin became Nina Biornsen; I chose my uncle's name, because he is dead."

"Dead! Is Andrei Bernin dead?"

"Yes, he died at Moscow on the fourteenth of November, 1916."

Maurice Wallion looked inquiringly at Lona Ivanovna, and she replied to his unspoken question.

"My brother left the Copper House in January, 1916, for a reason which I will tell you by and by. For the same reason, Sonia and I allowed our friends to believe that he was still here, but too ill to see anyone. No one suspected the truth; I made for myself the disguise which Sergius is wearing now, and on two occasions I purposely allowed Baron Fayerling's spies to get a glimpse of the sick man, who was believed to be, but really was not, here."

It did not occur to Wallion to smile at the grotesque idea of the old lady in a false beard and man's clothes: on the contrary, he found something touching and pathetic in what she had done; he understood that she had been driven to it by the direst necessity.

"It was a hard blow for us when my brother died," she continued. "He died secretly in the country which had rejected him. My son has carried on his work, and now it is finished: but it has nearly cost him his life...."

She spoke slowly and composedly, and with a calm dignity which made Wallion feel that he was standing on holy ground; he fixed his gray eyes on her with a look of warm admiration.

"Then," he asked, "is your son—here?"

"Sergius is my son," she replied.

Wallion nodded; the discovery did not surprise him, since it had been one of his theories in the course of his attempts to arrive at the truth during the last few hours. He understood too, from Leo's expression, that this was the information which the young man had been so anxious to convey to him. But he was silent, for he could see that Lona Ivanovna had more to say. Presently she began again:

"I know you are our friend, Mr. Wallion; we can never forget how you saved Sergius yesterday, and today we have waited and hoped for you hour after hour. You must think it very strange that we should be in the Copper House, apparently at the beck and call of such creatures as Baron Fayerling and his companions; but you may find the explanation even more surprising. If you really are willing to help us, I will be perfectly frank with you, and tell you the whole story."

She spoke with a perceptible effort to keep to the point and to repress any display of emotion, which she would have considered a sign of weakness, but in spite of the quiet words, it was apparent that she was deeply moved. Sergius leaned forward and stroked her hand, and Wallion got up, shut the door into the hall, and said:

"Miss Sonia, as you are nearest, will you kindly look out, and tell me if you see anyone outside the window; I think it wisest not to show my face yet."

The girl complied; there was nobody outside: everything was quiet. Even the great barrier of dark thunder-clouds seemed motionless. Wallion looked round him once more with those keen eyes of his that nothing escaped; he missed something, and it struck him that the Austrian's calm, intelligent face would just have made their circle complete. But for the present, that was impossible.

Lona Ivanovna had seated herself beside her son, and waited for the journalist to follow her example. He understood her look, and readily obeyed it, saying with a smile:

"I am sure that between us we shall find a way out of all our difficulties: at any rate, I promise to do my best. I shall be delighted to hear your story, to begin with."

Lona Ivanovna took up her work-basket, which had been hanging neglected on her arm, remarking:

"I can think better when I am working," and as her crochet-needle flashed in and out of the stitches, she began her tale.

"Our father was a magistrate at Saratov. It was his wish that my brother should obtain a commission in the army, but as both our parents died early, we were left, whilst still quite young, to fend for ourselves. We had a little money, but not much, because my father, who had been sufficiently original not to make a fortune by means of bribery and corruption, had left nothing but debts behind him.

"We became students at Moscow, and you would scarcely believe how cleverly we and our companions managed to live upon nothing! It was a long time ago, in the days of Russia's slavery, and we youngsters hated the oppressors. You know what a struggle we made; and in the free countries around us the comfortable middle-classes sat still and called us anarchists! We were revolutionaries, and I, Lona Ivanovna, have risked my own life in active propaganda-work. My brother was weaker, and he served the cause with his pen, whilst I did so with words and deeds. We formed a little group of devoted enthusiasts, and there was one man who constituted himself a leader among us, constantly urging us on to fresh exertions. He became my husband, and Sergius is our son. The name of that man was Marcus Tassler."

"Marcus Tassler!" exclaimed Leo involuntarily, and with intense astonishment. Lona Ivanovna looked at him steadily, and he dropped his eyes and added confusedly:

"Forgive my interruption, but somehow that man's name surprised me more than anything else."

Wallion moved impatiently.

"Please go on," he murmured.

"Yes, I married Marcus Tassler," she went on calmly. "He was at that time a Russian subject, and we were just of an age. Perhaps he was not so worthless then: I don't know; we change with time. Several years passed; not all 'red,' but very often 'black' ones. I was imprisoned for the cause of liberty in Peter-Paul fortress. Then came 1905, that year of bloodshed and of barricades, with days of ardent enthusiasm, and of bitter disappointment; when the soldiers mutinied at Sevastopol, Poland was declared to be in a state of siege, and barricades were set up in the streets of Moscow. Can you imagine the horrors we went through? Spies and traitors were to be found, even amongst us…. One night our house was surrounded by Cossacks. My brother was there, Marcus Tassler, myself, and Sergius, who was then a boy of fourteen…."

"Fourteen!" echoed her son, "and I remember it all vividly: the wild faces, the whips cracking, the shooting—I remember it all."

"We were driven to prison like animals to the slaughter," she continued, "and we expected nothing else but death, for we were guilty of taking part in the December risings in Moscow. Then the examinations began: we were called in one by one. A fortnight later, a miracle happened! We were set at liberty, with no verdict, no conditions, no supervision. We returned to our comrades, and a terrible and inconceivable experience awaited us: they cast us out, accusing us of having purchased our freedom by treachery. We denied it indignantly. They reckoned up the names of all who had been shot, all who had been sent to Siberia—we were the only ones who had been set free. It was useless to protest, to ask for explanations, we were caught in a net, and they shrank from us as though we were pariahs…. We were even subjected to attacks from bombs, and it was due to one of these that Andrei lost his sight. That ended it. We were obliged to leave Russia, to escape from the vengeance of our former comrades. For private reasons, into which I need not enter now, I obtained a legal separation from Marcus Tassler—perhaps I unconsciously saw through him already—Sergius remained with me, and as exiles we sought sanctuary in Sweden. I haven't mentioned my brother's marriage; during a visit to Sweden in 1898, he had met and married Helena Flycht, a young half-Finnish, half-Swedish girl, who followed him to Russia. She died when Sonia was born, and the child was brought up by her mother's parents in Finland. Well, when Andrei, Sergius and I settled in Sweden, my brother sent for Sonia, and we were quite a little family party again. But the circle was soon broken. As Sergius grew up, the 'liberty-fever' developed in him, and he returned to Russia under an assumed name to take part in the work; for several years we heard no more of him."

"For a very good reason," interposed Sergius: "I was in prison the greater part of the time!"

"Then the World War began," Lona Ivanovna went on: "my brother made one attempt to offer his services to the revolutionaries. They answered us: 'Unless you can prove that you did not betray us in 1905, we will have nothing to do with you: we have forgotten nothing!' Prove it! How could we hope to do so now, if we had not succeeded at the time? We felt that we were excommunicated forever. Then Tassler reappeared. I had not heard a word of him for nine years, but now, in the spring of 1915, he came back. He undertook to prove our innocence of the accusation of treachery, upon one condition, that we in our turn, should help him. Bit by bit, he told us of a man called Gabriel Ortiz, who was planning a gigantic attempt to organize the Russian efforts for freedom. It sounded genuine, we should, at all events, be once more working for the cause of liberty, and that decided us. In the summer of 1915, we settled down here at the Copper House…Andrei, Sonia and I."

"Did Marcus Tassler really initiate you into Ortiz' plan?" asked Wallion, thoughtfully.

"Yes, into part of it, at any rate: that is to say, Baron Fayerling did. Part of the business was carried on here: smuggling arms, dispatching propagandist literature, and so forth. But we soon noticed that our part in it was a very small one; we were simply used as decoys, and all they wanted was Andrei's name on the contract and on their papers. Just at first we were satisfied, but we soon began to feel suspicious: it was too late for us to withdraw, and we found that we were practically prisoners here. We had no means of discovering what was really going on, but we had no intention of allowing ourselves to be involved in some fresh deed of treachery. It was then that we began to realize that Marcus Tassler was a dangerous character. We decided to obtain our own proofs, and we planned everything with the greatest precaution. In the spring of 1916, Andrei left the Copper House secretly, and traveled to Russia with a passport which I had managed to procure, and together with two revolutionaries who had still continued our friends. Meantime, Sonia and I gave out that my brother was lying ill in the Copper House, and no one suspected that he was far away! Besides, the baron and Tassler left us more and more to ourselves; it was enough for their purposes to have us here as figureheads. You can understand how anxious I was, when you think that Andrei was blind, and what a journey he had undertaken, and for what an object. I had a presentiment—but perhaps you don't believe in presentiments?"

"Yes," answered Wallion, "I certainly believe in them; a presentiment is often a subconscious conclusion, and may have a definite value."

"In January of this year, I received indirect information that my brother was dead. He had died quite suddenly of heart disease, unknown and alone in an infirmary at Moscow. Those were sad days for Sonia and me."

She stopped, for her voice was quivering suspiciously, and sat gazing before her, with her grimmest and most unapproachable expression; but Sonia understood, and nestled up more closely to her.

"The night is darkest before the dawn," began the old lady again. "Sergius sent us a letter, bidding us be of good courage; he had arrived too late to see his uncle alive, but had taken possession of his papers, and seen to the funeral. He wrote that he had made important discoveries...."

"Let me go on from there," said Sergius, turning towards the journalist. "I was staying in Moscow under the name of Dr. Zero. The March Revolution had changed everything, and my revolutionary friends were triumphant. I suspected that their rejoicings were rather premature, for I saw beneath the surface very definite symptoms of reactionary currents; I found proofs of the existence of a conspiracy, and Prince Tarraschin's death set me wondering.... Finally, after a series of researches, I heard of Tarraschin's memorandum, its contents, and the struggle that was being secretly carried on for its possession; in the long run, I also discovered its whereabouts: then I acted." He thought for a little while.

"You must remember that my motive all along has been the vindication of my own and my family's honor, also that I knew nothing of Ortiz, or of what was going on here; and lastly, that I dared not approach the new Russian government under my own name, as Kerensky had been one of those who had driven out Andrei and his belongings, branded as traitors. All this you must bear in mind.

"Well, I took Tarraschin's memorandum, not from its rightful owners, but from thieves. Of course, I know now, that it was from one of Ortiz's spies that I took it. But what was I to do with it? I had found my relatives' new address amongst my uncle's papers, and I determined to travel home and ask my mother's advice. On the way back, I fell in with B.22 and was very nearly caught in a trap...."

"I suppose your plan was to come here, and by the aid of the document, open negotiaions with Kerensky?" asked Wallion.

"Yes, it was the only way I could think of to regain the esteem of the revolutionaries."

"Doesn't it look a little bit like—bribery?"

Sergius Tassler was silent, and the journalist changed his tactics.

"Ah, well, of course you were justified in taking such a step. We know what happened afterwards, so...."

"Let me say one thing," said Sergius. "It is not fair to call it a bribe. I am prepared to surrender the paper unconditionally, but, by giving it up at the right moment, I want to add weight to the proofs I obtained in Moscow; I allude to the proofs of our innocence of the accusation brought against us in 1905."

"Really! You found them, then?"

"Yes, after the Revolution the police-archives became at last accessible, and there I found the name of the traitor; then everything became clear to me: my own father had played the part of Judas!"

"Marcus Tassler?"

"Yes, he was an infamous spy, and only allowed himself to be arrested for the sake of appearances, to escape any reprisals. He was, I suppose, driven by his uneasy conscience to bring about our liberation. But through him, hundreds of brave young students had gone to their death, or to Siberia; and that was my father...mine...."

Lona Ivanovna checked him....

"That's enough, my boy, don't let us talk of the man any more. You can understand now, Mr. Wallion, how, after Sergius' return yesterday, Tassler's double-dealing became perfectly clear to me. In 1905 he had made us accomplices in an act of treachery: what was his intention now? Why were we in the Copper House? It was evidently not enough for him that he had us outlawed twelve years ago; once again he must drag us down to destruction! Ever since the March Revolution, this year, I guessed that something was wrong, for Ortiz' activities did not diminish, although Russia was now freed. It was, therefore, not revolution, but something else that he was working for. The history of Tarraschin's memorandum revealed the truth in a flash. From the moment that Sergius told me about it, I became the enemy of Ortiz, and above all, of Tassler who had dared to lie to me."

"Tell me," said the journalist, "what exactly happened yesterday when your son arrived?"

"It all passed like a hurried dream. Suddenly, without any warning, he was here, with Rastakov at his heels. I had barely a second to decide what to do, and I did it. I sent him up with Sonia to Andrei's room, to disguise himself as my brother, whom Rastakov was quite prepared to see in the course of his investigations; I remained in the hall, and when I heard Rastakov coming, I fired a shot, to mystify him, and gain time: a shot always entails explanation and discussion, doesn't it?"

"So that's the true story of Bernard Jenin's disappearance?" said Wallion, amused.

"Yes, Bernard Jenin will never be found now!"

Wallion got up, walked up and down for a minute, and stopped before Sergius, sitting quiet and aloof, in his apparent blindness.

"And what about Tarraschin's memorandum?" he asked.

"It is hidden in a place where Rastakov would never dream of looking for it," answered Sergius; "in fact, it is actually in my hand at the present moment: look here, I will show it you."

All eyes were turned, as by common consent, on Sergius' right hand, in which he was holding his stick. With a quick wrench, he unscrewed the ivory handle, and they saw that the stick was hollow; without looking into it, he handed it to the journalist.

"Will you be so kind?" said he; "the most important document in Europe will be found inside, rolled up like a cigarette! Don't stand on ceremony, please."

The journalist stretched out his hand, then drew it suddenly back; a curious expression came into his eyes, and he thrust his hands into his pockets.

"You are joking, surely, sir!"

"I? Certainly not. What do you mean?"

"There is nothing in the stick!"

Sergius Tassler grew pale, and stared, as though petrified, into the hollow tube. Lona Ivanovna bent forward, and as the stick fell with a thud on the floor, she said:

"Are you perfectly sure you put the paper in there yesterday?"

"Yes," he replied with a stupefied air; "I can't understand…. Sonia saw it…."

The young girl sprang forward like a little fury:

"I saw you put the paper in the stick! Nobody else saw it, nobody knows about it. Where is the document?" Her tone was almost an accusation, but Sergius made no reply. His mother continued her work with undisturbed equanimity, only remarking:

"You see, Mr. Wallion, that Tarraschin's memorandum is still capable of providing us with a sensation."

"So it seems. I am sorry, for I should have liked to have your only weapon in my hands."

"Our only weapon!" she echoed.

"Yes, without it, one doesn't know what may happen."

"Could Rastakov have taken it?" suggested Leo.

"Impossible," returned Sergius. "He hasn't even set eyes upon the stick, and the baron said openly that their search had been unsuccessful; it is a complete mystery to me…."

"Did you keep watch last night?" asked Wallion.

"Yes, all night, in turns."

"And you noticed nothing unusual?"

"Nothing whatsoever."

"Had you disturbed the contents of the stick since yesterday?"

"No, and I have never let it out of my sight."

The journalist examined it cursorily, screwed on the handle, and restored it to its owner.

"Well, there you are!" said he. "You may console yourself with the reflection that Ortiz would certainly never have suspected the existence of such a highly-original hiding-place."

"Console myself? Do you attach so little importance to the disappearance of the paper?" exclaimed the mortified and astonished Sergius.

"No, not that, but I have an idea that it has not gone beyond recall. The person who took it...."

"But who can it be? Who?"

"That remains to be seen. May I be allowed to examine Andrei Bernin's bedroom with you?"

"Most willingly."

Sergius and Lona Ivanovna followed him upstairs, but they all three returned very soon. Leo and Sonia, who were left sitting silent and downcast, saw an expression in the journalist's face which they could not quite fathom; it seemed almost as though he was quietly pleased about something which nobody else had observed.

"Have you found out anything?" Leo asked, in a low tone.

"No," replied Wallion, abstractedly; "nothing that I didn't already know."

After a minute he left the room.

* * * *

An oppressive silence lay heavy and stifling over the Copper House. Premature darkness had set in; the massive thunder clouds seemed to settle slowly down upon the woods and the lonely house, till they shut out the last rays of fading daylight.

Leo found the journalist at a window on the second floor, gazing out to sea. His whole bearing was tense with expectation, and his gray eyes dark and fixed. Leo wondered what he saw there, and placed himself silently beside him. From this place they had an uninterrupted view of the little bay, which lay gleaming inside its sheltering island.

Two men were busy with something spread out on the deck of the lighter; it appeared to be part of some apparatus; Wallion watched them intently.

"What is it?" whispered Leo.

His friend did not reply.

Suddenly a cone of bluish light darted up into the dusk as a result of the exertions of the two distant figures, and continued to burn with a steady and far-reaching beam. The ray of light shifted hither and thither, till it remained stationary between the islands and the right shore of the bay, pointing towards the open sea.

"The light!" murmured Wallion. "Ortiz is at hand!"

Part III—Gabriel Ortiz

CHAPTER XV

The Storm Bursts

A gust of wind went soughing through the trees, which bowed their crests before it in long, rippling lines. On the dark horizon, lightning flashed in and out of the dense bank of clouds, and the windows rattled as the peals of thunder sounded nearer and more frequent.

Then, from some way off, a short, sharp cry was heard through the rising storm. Men's steps came crashing through the bushes, and suddenly two shots rang out. Inside the Copper House, all sprang to their feet, and looked apprehensively at one another, with the conviction that the critical moment had arrived.

Wallion ran noiselessly downstairs, with Leo after him, and saw Lona Ivanovna crossing the hall, a revolver in her hand. Sonia had rushed to the glass door and was gazing out into the twilight: Sergius Tassler stood in the entrance to the dining-room, with one hand in his pocket.

"Someone is climbing over the balustrade of the terrace," said the girl suddenly, "and he has a revolver!"

"Who is it?" inquired Lona Ivanovna.

"I can't see yet—it's a man. Now he's turning round again."

Another revolver-shot cracked and was answered by the report of a gun further off. The revolver was fired once more, four shots in quick succession; hasty steps sounded on the gravel, and the girl started back from the door, as a shadow appeared just outside it, groping for the handle.

Wallion threw the door open, and a man ran right into his arms. It was Rosenthal, hatless, and with his coat torn.

"They discovered me," he panted, "shut the door, they are coming!"

Wallion did so, and returned to him, saying:

"What have you done?"

The Austrian began to reload his Browning.

"I went down to the lodge to telephone," said he.

"Well?"

"I got through to the *Daily Courier*, but Robert Lang was not there."

"Then, of course, you haven't spoken to him."

"No, I had no luck," said the Austrian stolidly; "and the worst of it was, that while I was standing at the telephone, the baron and Marcus Tassler returned from the station in a motorcar, and caught me. Fayerling spotted me at once, and raised the alarm. I tried to hold my ground, but was obliged to give in at last. Unfortunately, this puts an end to anything I could do as Rosenthal the gardener, so from now on, I become instead Max Raebel, the Austrian government detective, at your service, ladies and gentlemen."

He bowed to the assembled company.

A step of an entirely different kind was now heard on the gravel: light, firm, almost arrogant in its character.

It was Baron Fayerling, who tried the handle and shook the glass door. He was alone, and at a sign from the journalist, Lona Ivanovna went forward and opened the door.

"What do you want?" she demanded, looking him fearlessly in the face.

"I am not looking for you," replied the baron hastily: "I want that spy...."

"Would you not rather talk to me?" suggested Wallion, pushing Max Raebel on one side, and stepping forward.

The two men looked at one another. The baron raised his eyebrows, but his impassive face betrayed no other sign of surprise, though Wallion observed with considerable satisfaction, that he hesitated a little over his reply.

"So you are tired of playing hide and seek?" he said at length. "I'm afraid you must have found it very uncomfortable."

"Not in the least, baron, but I was beginning to fear that you had forgotten me."

The baron looked round, as though he meditated raising an alarm, and Wallion added quickly:

"Won't you come in? Perhaps you have something to say to me?"

"No, not yet. I suspected that you were here, when you were found to have been out of Stockholm for a whole day. Our business will keep. I presume that you have realized your mistake by this time?"

"In coming here, you mean? On the contrary, I made a great mistake in not coming sooner; it would have spared both you and myself a lot of trouble."

The baron looked narrowly at him.

"You should not have ventured here without a strong force!" he remarked.

"No, thanks, I prefer fair play."

"You don't lack self-confidence; I could tell that yesterday, from your letter, which I have kept."

"Ah, as a keepsake, no doubt!"

"No, to hand it over to my superior officer!" and the baron turned away, and left the room.

"What have you gained by that?" whispered Leo; "the fellow was white with rage."

"Did you notice that he absolutely ignored Max Raebel?" answered the journalist; "I think we shall still be left in peace for a bit."

"Not for long, though," Lona Ivanovna put in, pointing towards one of the windows that faced seawards, from which they saw the reflection of the blue light over the tops of the trees.

"It's coming at last, is it?" murmured Wallion, and he went upstairs three steps at a time, followed by Leo who guessed that he was returning to his post of observation. When they reached the window overlooking the shore, they saw that almost total darkness had set in. Long shadows, and floods of bluish-white light drifted alternately across the mirror-like surface of the bay, and only the dim outline of the lighter could be distinguished.

"Now you are going to see something which will surprise you," said a voice behind Leo: it was that of the Austrian, who had followed them upstairs.

"Yes," Wallion chimed in, almost gaily, "if I am not mistaken, we may look for Gabriel Ortiz at any minute now!"

The journalist was worked up to a high pitch of excitement; he was evidently in his element at the near prospect of a good tussle: a faint flush mounted to his cheeks, and his eyes sparkled: he was smoking continuously.

Leo's eyes were fixed on the channel between the islands and the shore, and there he saw something which made him suddenly grip the window-ledge. In the center of the flood of light, something seemed to be moving on the surface of the water: a spar had shot right up out of the sea and was approaching the lighter at an astounding rate. It seemed to increase in height as it came nearer, and presently, out of the foaming water there appeared a turret, and a convex shining mass, like the back of a whale.

"What is that?" he exclaimed; "why—but that's impossible!" The beam of light followed the extraordinary object, which was now slackening speed very noticeably: a hatchway was seen to open, and men's figures began to emerge from the turret, which was still streaming wet from its immersion.

"It's too absurd!" cried Leo, staring harder than ever; "a submarine! I don't understand...."

"Why, what an unbelieving fellow you are!" growled the Austrian. "Can't you see for yourself...."

"Yes, but...when you come to think of it...a submarine!"

"Well, it's evident that nothing less will do for Gabriel Ortiz. Of course, that's his flagship. Surely you didn't expect him to come in a rowing-boat!"

Wallion smiled.

"Did you know it?" demanded Leo quickly.

"Yes," replied the journalist. "I guessed as much, when I saw how the side of the lighter was damaged. The Russian submarine fleet has practically gone the way of all flesh: half of it blown up, and the remainder surrendered. Why shouldn't one or two of them have been simply stolen? You can't deny that Ortiz is a man who knows how to make the most of his opportunities. It is really a brilliant idea! He always ran a certain amount of risk with the motor-launch 'Nelly,' but with this one, he is never obliged to 'lie-to' and answer inconvenient questions from the coastguards. There they go, bang against the lighter!"

The three spectators now heard a subdued creaking, and the flare on board the lighter was extinguished. A sharp order was given, and in a few minutes, a less powerful light appeared, and began to move backwards and forwards. The respective silhouettes of the lighter and the submarine were merged into one; a little yawl approached the ruined pier, and several lanterns began to twinkle like glowworms. They were arranged in a row on the beach, and by their light a party of six or eight men could be seen, starting up the path that led to the Copper House. At the same time, voices, amongst which they recognized the baron's, were heard in excited conversation beneath the window: the arrival of the submarine had been discovered.

At the head of the little band, walked a solitary undersized figure, in a flapping waterproof: it was obvious who this must be.

"That's the man!" said the Austrian, in a low voice: "that's Ortiz!"

As if the powers of the air had been waiting for this announcement, the storm now burst upon them in earnest. An unusually dazzling glare of violet lightning spread a network of phosphorescent light over the whole extent of the blue-black sky, and as it faded out, a peal of thunder crashed over the house like an avalanche, till the walls seemed to shake, and the floors to rock. The rain fell in torrents, pouring down in one continuous cascade; when the echo of the thunder at length died away, the noise of the rain took its place, and the drops pattered against the panes and the roof like machine-gun fire after the heavy artillery has ceased.

But nothing stopped the progress of the little band. The three men who were watching them could see through the veil of rain the solitary figure marching along at their head, the cape of his waterproof fluttering like black wings about his shoulders.

"Well," said Wallion, "our ally is rather late in arriving, but has come at all events. Come along…."

"Our ally?" echoed Raebel.

"Yes, the storm. It deprives them of sight and hearing for the time being. Let's go downstairs."

They went down again, and joined the three Bernins, who were silently awaiting them in the dark dining-room.

"Now for it!" said the journalist, gathering them all round him. "Quick's the word, and sharp the action! Sergius Tassler, whatever happens, you must continue to play the part of Andrei Bernin as long as it can be kept up —and you, Lona Ivanovna, must stand by him. Above all, we must do nothing rashly: our chief aim is to gain time. I propose to remain here and meet the first brunt of Ortiz' attack: I think I shall be able to give him plenty to think about! But you, gentlemen," turning to Leo and Raebel, "you must make a last attempt to run the blockade: one or other of you will, in all probability be able to get through. Do anything you like, steal the baron's car, or fight your way to the station, but get word to Robert Lang of the arrival of the submarine, and instruct him to take immediate steps to capture the whole gang."

"Yes, yes," answered Leo eagerly, "we ought to have thought of that long ago!"

"Thought! I have thought of little else!" said Wallion impatiently. "But can't you see, that the rain and the darkness have given us our chance?"

"That's clear," interposed the Austrian, "so don't let's waste time in talking."

He went to a window, and opened it without a sound; the darkness outside rose up like a wall in front of him. As Leo was following him, he felt a hand on his arm: it was Sonia.

"Let me come too!" she whispered.

Wallion, who overheard her, was on the point of refusing, but Lona Ivanovna said:

"Let the child go, she can look after herself better than any boy!"

The journalist, moved by the pleading in the girl's eyes, gave in to the old lady, and offered no opposition, the more so, as every minute's delay was dangerous. Sonia had changed into her black riding costume, probably in the expectation of some such contingency, and was already at the window; to Leo's whispered attempt to dissuade her, she only replied with a shake of the head.

"Be off, then, at once, all three of you," said Wallion briskly; "don't stop, whatever happens; if one of you gets through, lose no time in getting in touch with the nearest authorities; knock people up, telephone to Stockholm, do everything you can…."

He continued to whisper his instructions to them, whilst he was helping them to get through the window. They were eager to start off, and carry out their orders, and the storm seemed to swallow them up in a moment. It was like being thrown into the sea. The rain lashed their faces, and the wind tore at their clothes, but the three adventurers summoned up all their courage, bent their heads, and began to cross the terrace.

Darkness had obliterated the big house behind them, they could not hear their own footsteps, and groped their way onwards, afraid of losing one another. Sheets of rain enveloped them: it was impossible to see or hear the sentries, who must certainly be near them; but this they had to risk.

"This way," said Leo, just above his breath.

They were brought up short by the stone balustrade, over which they scrambled, jumping down on to the grass. At that instant, the sky was lit up by a flash, broad and blue as a stream of molten silver. For one second, they, the trees and the bushes, stood out distinctly, then the darkness wrapped them round again, and they were deafened by the succeeding peal of thunder. Leo seized Sonia's hand, and dragged her along with him: an alarming sight had met their eyes; crouching under the shelter of the trees were a number of sentries, their hoods pulled up over their heads, and their guns under their waterproof capes. The fugitives had been seen. A shrill whistle was audible through the dying reverberations of the thunder, and lanterns appeared at various points. The darkness protected them for a moment, but they dreaded the next flash. The lights seemed to move more rapidly, and voices called out questions and answers. Leo and the girl ran on wildly through the wet grass; suddenly a rough voice shouted something quite close to them, and a lantern was flashed into their faces. Before the young man knew what was happening, he found himself engaged in a hand-to-hand combat; his left hand grasped a rifle-barrel, his right, a wet and twisted collar. A shot rang out, and a red flame seemed to flash just below his elbow: using his knee as a lever, he bent the gun across it, wrenched it free, and flung it away. His panting assailant, whose breath reeked of bad tobacco, seized him by the shoulders and tried to force him down, but Leo got the fellow round the waist, lifted him off the ground, and they rolled over together. His clenched fist came in contact with a chin, and he received several kicks from feet tramping backwards and forwards. He sprang up, caught hold of someone, who swore violently, and hurled him far in amongst the bushes, just as another flash lighted up the landscape. The vivid glare showed him the Austrian struggling with three men at once.

"They've got me!" Raebel cried; "see to yourself!"

Leo turned to find yet another adversary, gave him a stinging blow on the ear, and dodged past him into the shelter of the trees. Somebody made a grab at his foot, but he kicked it loose, and after a minute's frantic rush through soaking wet branches and leaves, which slapped him in the face, he found himself on level ground, drew a deep breath, and realized that he was in the avenue. Had he actually broken through the cordon of sentries? It seemed almost impossible, but without stopping to puzzle it out, he sped on down the avenue. He fancied he could hear light footsteps running a little ahead of him; it was Sonia, and he called out softly to her. But what was this? She was running towards him: was she turning back? They stopped opposite one another.

"Why have you turned back?" he panted; "are they in front of us?"

"No, no," she whispered eagerly; "it is you...if you go in this direction...it's you that are making a mistake...look, look!"

Sure enough, Leo noticed to his dismay that in the darkness he had taken a wrong turn. Through the trees in front of them, he now saw the terrace steps, full of lights and men. The little party from the boat were just marching up the path from the bay, and the short figure in the waterproof was ascending the steps, at a brisk, steady pace. Someone held a lantern in front to guide him, and by its light they saw his pale, determined face, looking upwards and onwards, as though he intended to allow nothing to turn him from his purpose.

Then Leo and Sonia turned and fled, without looking behind them. Gabriel Ortiz' face had terrified them by its indomitable strength, and they realized that all was lost, unless they succeeded in obtaining help. Stumbling along through the pools of water, they hurried on faster and faster.

CHAPTER XVI

Gabriel Ortiz Musters His Forces and Counts His Prisoners

Maurice Wallion remained at the window for some little time. The lightning had shown him the terrace empty: would the three messengers succeed in getting past the sentries? He was quivering all over with excitement....

Ah, what was that! That ominous whistle must mean that someone had seen them. There was a flash through the darkness as a shot was fired; he leaned out, and heard a confused noise among the trees, where lights now began to dance like will o' the wisps.

Lona Ivanovna, at his elbow, gave a little gasp.

"That was a shot," she said; "what is wrong out there?" The lights clustered together, then shifted rapidly from one spot to another.

"Hark, that's the Austrian's voice: it sounds as though they had caught him...but the others! Sonia!" she whispered anxiously; "if only we could see!"

They held their breath, but now nothing could be heard except the swish of the rain, and most of the lights had disappeared.

"They've done it!" said Wallion. "I believe they have got through." He closed the window, and went out into the hall.

"Our part of the task remains to be done," he added; "look, there comes the procession, but without its band and colors. This begins to get exciting! I wonder in which character the great man will appear tonight: emperor or millionaire?"

He posted himself just inside the glass doors, and watched with calm interest the spectacle outside. It was really, as he said, a regular procession that was advancing, though at present, one could only distinguish a line of shadowy forms, interspersed with flickering white lights.

Five of Rastakov's men ran first up the terrace steps, and took up their position at some distance from one another; they were followed by Rastakov himself, calling out a series of orders in Russian. A minute later, the whole terrace was illuminated by the powerful glare of four acetylene lights, carried by as many torch-bearers, who halted at the top of the steps, and looked round them expectantly: other shadows were visible behind them.

The short, upright figure in the waterproof now marched up the steps, with Baron Fayerling on his left: his every movement was firm and unhesitating. The baron was speaking: he was evidently giving his report, to which the Chief listened without stopping, without answering, without looking at his companion. Close behind them came six men, wearing the uniform of marines, and armed with cutlasses and carbines.

"Look at his bodyguard!" murmured the journalist; "the great man doesn't trust himself entirely to his friends: one might almost imagine...."

He broke off. The torch-bearers had shifted their position a little, and the bright light fell directly on Ortiz' face. From that moment, Wallion no longer saw anything ridiculous about his antagonist; he was obliged to admit (like everyone else who had been brought into contact with this man), that the first glimpse of Ortiz' face made a remarkable impression upon him; its look of intense concentration fascinated him; the man's whole self seemed bent on the attainment of an all-embracing, all-absorbing, and as yet unrealized ambition. His face was pale, but expressive of unlimited strength of will; the mouth small, straight, thin-lipped, and unsmiling; the eyes, which were deep set and penetrating, seemed to look far beyond their immediate surroundings into some boundless realm of fancy, bright with the promise of power and sovereignty; and from their depths shone the unquenchable conviction which is the hall-mark of the fanatic.

"Do you see him?" whispered Lona Ivanovna.

"Yes," answered the journalist; "I see that I have made a miscalculation."

"What did you expect?"

Wallion did not answer. What exactly had he expected? A caricature of Napoleon? A common adventurer, acting a ridiculous part? No, and yet he had perhaps unconsciously hoped that Gabriel Ortiz should turn out to be —just the "Emperor of the Amazons." But the antagonist who at length presented himself, after months of suspense, was no comic hero—he was a man! A man who, in deadly earnest, was bent on fulfilling his dearest ambition in defiance of law and order—and between him and his ambition stood only one obstacle—Maurice Wallion.

"What a fight it will be," said the journalist aloud; "one of us must go under!" He breathed hard, and clenched and unclenched his fists.

"Now!" whispered Lona Ivanovna.

The group on the terrace advanced again; Baron Fayerling had finished talking, and stepped on one side. Gabriel Ortiz was walking towards the house, his head bent, and his hands clasped behind him. Suddenly he looked up, and said sharply:

"Who are in the house?"

The baron's reply was inaudible, but Wallion was sure that he only mentioned three names, as he made a gesture towards the dark garden. Ortiz nodded shortly. Lona Ivanovna remarked, from her place by Wallion's side:

"If only I had that baron's throat between my fingers!"

He hushed her with a look, and drew her back from the door as she was on the point of sallying forth.

"You must keep as cool as ice!" he warned her; "you will want all your wits, all your cunning now. Our aim is to gain time, not to indulge in heroics; put away your revolver, it would only make matters worse."

She replaced the weapon reluctantly in her workbag, and they withdrew silently.

At a signal from the baron, the lights were turned upon the entire front of the house, shining right into the windows; slanting, flickering shafts of light illuminated the hall, and just as Lona Ivanovna and the journalist were leaving it, the locked doors yielded to a violent push, showers of glass tinkled over the oak floor, and the walls echoed to the steady tramp of men.

"Lights on everywhere!" ordered the baron. "Put a man at every door; you two stop here."

Steps approached the dining-room: the curtain that screened it from the hall, was pulled aside with a rattle, and Ortiz appeared in the doorway.

He looked coolly and critically at the persons who awaited him; then he came in, still accompanied by the baron. Two of the men in uniform stood on guard by the door, and two others placed their lamps on the mantelpiece, filling the room with a dazzling light, in which faces appeared unnaturally pale, and shadows unnaturally dark. There was silence for an instant: Ortiz, his hands still behind him, signed to his adjutant to draw back a little, that he might speak. His deep, piercing glance travelled from the white-haired form in the armchair to Lona Ivanovna's upright figure, and finally rested upon Wallion. He seemed to be looking down upon them from a great height, taking stock of everything, and coördinating all details into one complete whole.

But the journalist, who was growing impatient, could not deny himself the satisfaction of the first word.

"Good evening, Gabriel Ortiz. I have long wished to meet you; dare I hope that Baron Fayerling will introduce me?"

Ortiz unfastened his dripping waterproof, and threw his hat on a chair.

"It is not necessary, Maurice Wallion: I know you already."

"And my—friends?" asked the journalist, emphasizing the word "friends," and waving his hand towards Lona Ivanovna and the sick man. "Do you...?"

"I know them also."

Ortiz' reply was short and sharp. His expression changed as he looked at the journalist: it evinced more hostility but at the same time, more interest than before, and he added:

"Do you count them among your friends? That is risky; I am sorry that you have come here, Maurice Wallion."

"Would it not be more to the point if you explained by what right you invade the Copper House in this brutal way?"

"By the strongest right!"

"You are on Swedish soil: let me remind you of its laws."

"I have my own."

"In other words, you are an outlaw."

"From your point of view—not from mine."

"Do you depend so much upon our being helpless?"

"No, I depend only upon myself. I have not come here to make terms: your point of view does not interest me. I have come to get Tarraschin's memorandum."

"Are you sure that it exists?"

"Yes, for what else could you offer in exchange?"

"In exchange for what?"

"Your life."

Ortiz uttered these two words in a perfectly ordinary tone, but his deep-set eyes remained somber and remote; his inmost thoughts seemed to have strayed into that far-off region where his future lay hidden. Wallion realized that to this dark and dangerous being, one life signified less than nothing, but he said quietly:

"You are too hasty; threats are not a sign of strength."

Ortiz turned away without answering him.

"A table and a chair!" he commanded. The two men hastened to obey, and placed what he asked for in the middle of the room; he seated himself, and the baron took up his position close by.

Wallion remained on the alert for any sounds from outside. By this time, the three messengers ought to have solved their problem. No sound issued from the darkness that surrounded the house; the rain had abated, and there were longer intervals between the flashes of lightning. Was it possible that all three had got safely away?

"I miss three of your friends," said Ortiz suddenly; "where are they?"

"Do you wish to see them?"

"I do."

"Then I regret that I can give you no information about them."

Ortiz laid a paper on the table in front of him. It was covered with names and dates; he ran his pen down the lines, making a mark against three of them: finally he looked up.

"Rosenthal, gardener. Bring the man in, Baron Fayerling."

The baron went to the door, a scuffle was heard in the hall, and, panting and dishevelled, a drenched figure was hustled up to the table: it was the Austrian.

"Look at me," said Ortiz coldly. "Are you Rosenthal?"

"Yes," replied the gardener hoarsely.

"You were engaged on the recommendation of Madame Sumensov, on the 29th of April?"

"Yes."

"You have made two attempts to betray us today; what have you to say for yourself?"

The Austrian was silent.

"Have you nothing to say?"

"No."

"Can you deny that you are an Austrian detective named Max Raebel?" said Ortiz.

The Austrian laughed bitterly:

"No, I am glad you know it," he replied. "It doesn't matter now; I have done with you and your associates in Russia; you may do your worst…."

Ortiz seemed to ignore this remark; he made a sign to the baron, pointed to the paper, and said a few words in an undertone. The baron shrugged his shoulders:

"That's impossible!" he replied with a contemptuous glance at the Austrian. Ortiz got up, went across to the detective, and looked him straight in the face.

"You have been here two months," said he, reflectively; "have you made any notes?"

"Do you think so little of me as to ask me that?" retorted Raebel. "I never take notes, but I have a good memory…."

"What is your memory worth?"

Raebel did not reply.

"A million, perhaps?"

"No. Do you wish me to name my terms?"

"Yes."

"Give me Tarraschin's memorandum, surrender yourself to the authorities, and distribute your millions among the poor, and I may consider the matter!"

Ortiz turned his back upon him, returned to the table, and said, without raising his voice:

"See that this fellow is taken on board, when we leave here."

"Would it not be better to do it at once?" suggested the baron.

"No, I might require him again. Isn't Rastakov ready yet?"

"Yes, he's just coming."

Rastakov entered the room.

"Well!" Ortiz greeted him.

"I have searched Rosenthal's room," replied Rastakov; "he has made no notes, and I have found nothing."

"Good!"

Ortiz sat silent for a little time. It did not escape Wallion that the baron and Rastakov exchanged a rapid glance full of uneasiness; he could guess the reason.

Ortiz looked at his watch.

"Rastakov—have you left any of your men in Stockholm?"

"No, they are all here."

"Nobody missing?"

"No."

"Is everything aboard the lighter?"

"Yes."

"Good!" said the Chief once again. "Bring in Leonard Grath and Sonia Bernin immediately; I don't wish to wait any longer."

The baron bit his lips and looked nervously at Rastakov. For several seconds a dead silence reigned in the room, at the end of which Rastakov went out, making an ambiguous sign to Fayerling.

"Well!" said Ortiz, raising his voice, and looking round him. "Where is Rastakov gone? What does this mean? Am I not to be obeyed?"

Max Raebel had drawn close to Wallion, and said rapidly in a barely audible voice:

"They caught me almost directly, but I played my part for all it was worth, I can tell you! Three of them seized me at once and dragged me down, but I believe the youngsters got away safely."

Ortiz fixed his dark eyes upon them, and exclaimed sharply: "Gentlemen! You had better speak out loud; nobody whispers in my presence. Can either of *you* perhaps inform me where the two missing persons are to be found?"

Wallion replied:

"They have gone to fetch some friends of mine, who might otherwise arrive too late to meet you.…."

Ortiz' eyes blazed; this time he was visibly provoked, and patches of red appeared on his cheeks.

"So that is what you are waiting for! I saw through you from the first; you are at the bottom of all this. You must be a very optimistic man, Maurice Wallion, if you imagine that I have not anticipated your action. Do I need to tell you that nothing can stop me?"

He struck the table with the palm of his hand.

"I am the master of Copper House for tonight, and I intend to show it! You have sent them to alarm the authorities? That is a good move: but do you suppose that Rastakov would be such a fool as to admit them? And if he did, what would be the result? When the authorities get here, they will find no one to tell them what has occurred. I sweep clean after me, as you ought to know, after seeking me for so long."

"Brooms don't always sweep quite clean enough!" answered Wallion; "to begin with, how do you know that the runaways have not taken Tarraschin's memorandum with them, as literature for the journey?"

This shot struck home. Ortiz walked up to the journalist, and looked at him intently.

"If you have dared to do that!" said he, slowly; "but no, it is impossible. You couldn't be so foolishly reckless!"

He turned to Lona Ivanovna, who met his eyes without flinching.

"I know you, Lona Ivanovna! For you, and for him there," and he nodded contemptuously at the silent figure crouched in the armchair, "the document is altogether too costly!"

He swung round on his heel.

"Baron Fayerling! What are you waiting for? If there is such delay in bringing in my prisoners, I must take more vigorous measures."

The baron bowed low.

"I believe they are on the way here," he answered.

The Austrian seized Wallion by the arm:

"Hark, I hear people coming up the avenue! Either they have been caught, or else...."

A noise outside became audible. The journalist looked out of the window, and saw a dozen lanterns coming up the avenue, in whose light the dark faces of a band of men were visible; rifle-barrels gleamed, and a voice shouted:

"Are you all here? In with you, there is no time to lose!"

A crowd of men surged into the hall.

CHAPTER XVII

Leo and Sonia Determine to Steal a Motorcar but Fall Into an Unexpected Trap

Never before had Leo found the avenue between the Copper House and Karka gates so interminably long. Sometimes it seemed as wide as a boulevard, at others no broader than a woodland path, where he kept on bumping into the trees, and grazing his hands. The rain, which blew in diagonal lines across their path, or fell upon their heads in heavy drops from the thick foliage, drenched, but did not cool him; hot and breathless, he stumbled continually, and at last stood still, perfectly bewildered.

"Wait!" he panted to the young girl. "It has never taken me more than six minutes to walk down this avenue, but tonight it seems by some sort of black magic to be five times longer than usual. If one could at least see one's own nose!"

"Hush!" whispered Sonia. "We are somewhere near the lodge; I fancied I saw a light…."

Leo started nervously.

"Is there someone behind us?" he exclaimed, trying to peer between the trees. But he could no longer see even the lights on the terrace, and came to the conclusion that they must somehow have traversed the entire length of the avenue.

"No, it's nobody," said the girl, after listening for a minute; "they are too busy now with Ortiz' arrival."

"Ortiz! Don't speak of him, I am scared to death when I think of his face: supposing he comes after us!"

"No, no," said the girl, catching hold of his coat. "Never mind Ortiz now! Look, isn't that a light over there?"

They went on through the trees; a flash of lightning flickered through the darkness, but its momentary glimmer was not sufficient to show them their exact whereabouts; it was succeeded by a brief peal of thunder, echoing among the surrounding hills. Leo could see nothing of the light which the girl had noticed.

"Yes, yes!" she insisted; "it was just as though somebody was lighting a pipe—ah, there it is again!"

This time they really saw a faint glow, which threw an intermittent light upon a brutal face, wreathed in smoke, whilst a burning match ricochetted through the air and went out. Leo recognized the face of the gate-keeper Tugan, who had fired at him on his first arrival at the Copper House.

They heard him grumbling to himself, and suddenly a light flared out again: the man had opened a dark-lantern and was flashing it suspiciously first on one side, then on the other, but without discovering the fugitives, who had taken cover behind the trunk of a large tree. After some minutes the light vanished, and they thought they heard steps moving away. Meanwhile, the temporary illumination had shown them where they were: the lodge was not more than twenty paces away from them, and twenty paces further on to the right, they could make out the bars of the gates. The gate-keeper seemed to be the only human being about.

"He has gone," whispered Sonia. "He went out of the gate."

"No," returned Leo, "he went inside: I heard a door shut."

"Impossible, for we should see a light in the window."

"Not necessarily; he would be on the look-out."

They wrangled obstinately, though in subdued tones, assured that the rain and the wind were sufficient to cover any sound they might make.

"Let us wait a few seconds, and we shall know for certain"; Leo proposed finally; "I don't feel quite comfortable about it; the old fox may be lying in wait."

They stood so close together, sheltering as best they could from the rain, that the girl's soft hair brushed his face, and he could feel the vibration of her hurried breathing. She was evidently strung-up to a high pitch of excitement, and her agitation communicated itself to him, making him feel strengthless and confused.

"Sonia," said he, taking her hand, "I may call you Sonia, mayn't I? Your fingers are like ice, are you very frightened? Things have gone rather well, so far."

"No," she answered in a low tone, not withdrawing her hand; "I am not frightened...."

He ventured to squeeze the little hand.

"You'll see, if once we can get safely out of this, it will be all right. We shall manage to outwit the lot of them, Ortiz and his myrmidons; he shan't hurt your people, and tomorrow a happier future will dawn...."

"There can be no future for me," she burst out mournfully, "unless, unless...."

"Yes, unless what? Tell me."

"Unless Sergius is saved. He runs the greatest risk of all, and if he dies...."

She broke off with a sob, and the sound struck Leo like a blow.

"Yes, of course, Sergius," he murmured. "Oh, that'll be all right. Sergius shan't be taken from you."

In spite of his brave words he was conscious of a feeling of exhaustion and disappointment, as he realized that he had been fixing his hopes on something that was quite out of his reach...no, it was best as it was... Sergius! So all her anxiety was for him. Ah well, perhaps it was the most suitable....

He pulled himself together.

"Come along!" he encouraged her; "let's go ahead to rescue Sergius."

They went up to the lodge, and tried to look in through the window.

"He isn't there," whispered the girl.

"No, so it seems," muttered Leo; "but which way did he go?"

"That doesn't matter, we needn't bother about him," she returned impatiently. "Don't you remember that the telephone is here? We must telephone for help."

"Yes, you are right, let us do so at once."

They skirted the wall, and approached the door. Leo turned the handle, found the door unfastened, and entered.

Something whizzed past him with an ominous sound, and struck the door-post with a crack: it was a knife.

"Ha!" cried the young man, "is that your game, you sneaking brute!"

The burly form of the gate-keeper loomed dimly just inside the door, and Leo flung himself unhesitatingly upon him, for he knew that it was a matter of life or death. His enemy seized him in a bear's hug, but he wriggled out of it, and planted his fist squarely in the center of the brutal face. The fellow reeled backwards, slipped his right hand behind him, and raised the butt of his gun over his head, with a furious bellow.

"Oh no, I have had enough of that gun of yours," said Leo; "I owe you something for yesterday. Tit for tat, you know. Now then, come on and get it! And there's another: and just one more!"

Tugan had counted too much on his brute strength; the young man's powerful onrush gave him no chance of inflicting his intended death-blow with the clubbed rifle; a smashing blow on the point of the chin knocked him off his feet, he fell backwards over chairs and table with a crash, and lay motionless.

Leo groped for the matches, and a tiny, flickering flame lighted up the room. Tugan was stunned, and lay like a pole-axed steer on the floor; Sonia stared at him in alarm.

"Is he dead?" she whispered.

"No, he will soon come to."

With a certain satisfaction, Leo reflected that he must now have re-gained the prestige which he had lost in her eyes by his sham fight with the Austrian. The match went out, but he struck another, and lighted a candle which stood on the table. The telephone became visible on the wall near the door, and a thrill of triumph went through him, as he picked up the re-ceiver. At last he had succeeded! In another minute their plight would be made known to the outside world, and help would be forthcoming.

"Hallo!" he shouted impatiently: "hallo! Now then, Exchange! Can't you answer? Are you all asleep there? Hallo, hallo!"

Sonia gave a cry and pointed to the wall.

"Look! The wires are cut! The telephone is useless!"

Leo saw that she was right: the cut wires were dangling down. With an exclamation of dismay, he flung away the receiver.

"It is dreadful," faltered Sonia; "it shows that they have no further need of it; they just want to secure themselves against being surprised. We are lost!"

"Not yet," muttered Leo, "not yet."

He extinguished the candle, and they hurried out again into the rain, which had come on more heavily. They looked around them, and Leo said:

"We must get out through the gates."

"It's the only way," she agreed, but broke off. "Oh, look, look! They're coming!" she whispered.

Leo glanced instinctively up the avenue. Far back amongst the great trees, lights began to be reflected in the puddles, and to throw fantastic, leaping shadows on the path. There seemed to be four or five lanterns, and their rapid movements showed that the men who carried them were run-ning.

Without a word, Leo made for the gates; they were just ajar, and creaked horribly as they were pushed open to let the fugitives through. Out on the high-road they could hear voices inside the park, giving the alarm. In the middle of the road, eight or ten steps away, stood a large car, quivering with the throbbing of its engine. Two fugitives in wet coats were crouching under the hood, but they sprang out, and their black shadows were clearly defined against the beams of the headlights.

"We must have this," said Leo, and he rushed forward ready to throw the two figures into the mud. He immediately recognized one of them to be Marcus Tassler; the other was, presumably, the chauffeur. The young man "saw red," and he cried:

"Ah, here is our excellent friend, our benefactor, the honest merchant! So you persist in hanging about here, sir! I suppose you carry about the mortgages in your pocket, to make quite sure that I am not running off with the securities for your cash. Come along, old boy!—you fat little Neb-uchadnezzar!—just come along, and I'll reckon up what I owe you!"

He advanced threateningly, and, with a bound, Tassler placed himself in safety on the other side of the car.

"The fellow is mad!" he yelled. "Shoot him! Knock him down!"

The chauffeur threw himself between them, with a spanner in his gloved hand. He was a little bit of a man, and Leo put both arms around his waist, lifted him up, in spite of his frantic struggles, and flung him across the road, where he disappeared with a splash. Tassler continued to shout and threaten from the further side of the car.

"Easy there, old boy!" said Leo. "I haven't time...."

Sonia had already clambered into the car, and he followed her. He threw himself down behind the wheel, and grasped it as eagerly as though it had been a life-buoy. It was a pleasant surprise to find that the car was a "Mercedes," such as he had frequently driven in California. He cast one more look through the gates, towards the avenue: the dancing lights had almost caught them up. He touched the starting-gear with a light and practiced hand, and the car began to purr gently, gave a slight jerk, and rolled forward, as the tires took a grip of the wet surface of the road.

Tassler tore open his coat, snatched out a little nickelled revolver, and—piff, piff!—a couple of bullets whizzed past them. "Bang!" a rifle replied from the avenue. The young man laughed aloud. Sonia looked at him with surprise, and with renewed interest: he seemed transformed. The fighting blood of the Graths had for a few short moments wakened into life in this last effeminate scion of the race. At that minute he would have marched up to a battery of machine-guns: his eyes sparkled, and his long, "artistic" hair seemed to stand out round his head like a halo. The car shot away, its fifty horse-power obedient to the touch of his hand: they were off on the road to freedom. The dazzling headlights illuminated the darkness for ten yards ahead of them, and made the wet road shine like polished marble. The trees bordering the road stood motionless, their boughs heavy with moisture. And still the rain streamed and splashed down on them, in a tepid, unceasing shower-bath: it gurgled in the ditches, and drummed on the glass wind-screen of the car.

"Au revoir, Marcus!" Leo shouted over his shoulder. His voice was drowned in a peal of thunder, but the girl clapped her hands.

"That's splendid!" she exclaimed delightedly. "They can't catch us! Where will you drive to?"

"First of all to the nearest usable telephone," he replied. "And then—well, I hope there may be some sort of police-station in this neighborhood, otherwise we must make straight for Stockholm; it's all plain sailing now."

"Do you know the way?"

"Don't I just! Like the inside of my pocket!"

His self-confidence had gone up a hundred percent., since he got his hands on the steering-wheel. He let out the car to its fullest extent, murmuring:

"Good old Mercedes!—it's up to you, now! Show what you can do!"

And almost at the same instant, as the car obeyed him, and shot out at full speed, with the dizzying rush of a torpedo—at that instant the catastrophe was upon them! Their triumph was changed into bitter disappointment, and now they understood why so few shots had been sent after them; it was not freedom, but a murderous trap that awaited them.

"The wretches!" cried Leo. "They mean to murder us!"

Across the road in front of them, they caught sight of a network of slender, gleaming, sharp-edged threads; they were steel wires, stretched like a barbed-wire entanglement from side to side. At the speed at which they were going, every one of these wires must meet them like a sword-blade: it was impossible to evade them, they were everywhere.

The steering-wheel spun round between the young man's convulsively-working fingers; the car leaped from the track, swung round on two wheels, gave a terrific lurch, and ran in under the trees to a distance of several feet. The whole dead-weight of the ponderous machine was flung crashing into the ditch. Leo was shot through the air, and fell with outspread arms, and a sickening thud, deep into a soft, water-logged swamp. He rolled over, felt the water spurt up under his arms, and struggled to his knees. Both the lamps of the car had been smashed, and impenetrable darkness surrounded him. Dizzy with the shock, he felt as though he were still falling, and, faint with terror, he managed to catch hold of a branch. At length his head cleared, and he remembered his companion; what had become of her?

"Sonia!" he called anxiously; "Sonia!"

He scrambled to his feet. A sharp pain in his left shoulder showed him that he had not escaped unhurt, but for the minute that seemed of little consequence.

"Sonia, Sonia, where are you?"

"Here!" answered a faint voice.

He took a few steps, and ran into her; she was on her feet, leaning against the trunk of a tree, and trying to bandage her right hand with her handkerchief.

"Are you hurt?" he asked. "Can you walk?"

"Yes," she replied; "it's only a scratch. What about you?"

"Nothing to speak of."

"Let's go on," she murmured, but tottered as she spoke, and fell into his arms. "My head is a little giddy—never mind me—go...."

He saw that she was on the point of fainting, lifted her up, and carried her down to the road.

"Put me down," she said in a weak voice: "I can walk; we must hurry."

The lights from the gates were already quite near; they came on like a swarm of flying gnats, and running footsteps splashed along the road. At the sight of the wrecked car, a great shout of savage laughter was raised, and a voice called out:

"Stay there, you two, or I shall shoot!"

They were surrounded, and rough hands caught hold of them. Marcus Tassler's breathless voice panted in the background:

"Keep a sharp look-out on them, and take them with you to the Copper House. That was a very short drive, wasn't it, my young friends! You haven't much fight left in you, have you?"

He came up, laughing and rubbing his hands. Leo's excitement had died away, his muscles relaxed, and he realized that he was beaten. Fate was against them. Without a word, he and the young girl walked back side by side to the gates, surrounded by eight or ten men who hustled them along with coarse jests. They were prisoners once more. As Leo took a last glance in the direction where their lost freedom awaited them, he saw a little bright light shine out and twinkle, a long way off. It seemed to come from one of the hills to the left of the road, about a mile or so away, and was probably a signal. He wondered idly what it meant, and took it for granted that it was exchanged between some of Rastakov's men, but turned listlessly into the avenue, too worn-out to think. He didn't care what happened now: he had done his best—and failed!

Yet when he remembered Gabriel Ortiz, whose face he had already seen for one terrifying moment, he shuddered. The girl murmured softly:

"Ortiz is waiting for us!"

CHAPTER XVIII

Tarraschin's Memorandum Changes Owners

Inside the Copper House, the atmosphere of suspense became more and more heavily charged; nobody quite knew the cause of the sounds which now reached them from the avenue. It was impossible to guess what Ortiz was thinking, for he had spread out a map on the table and was studying it carefully. Wallion could see that it was a map of the environs of the Copper House. Suddenly Ortiz looked up into the journalist's eyes, with a frown; at that moment he really looked uncommonly like the "Little Gray Corporal." With his sparse, straggling hair, his keen, rather preoccupied glance, his small mouth, and round but determined chin, he was an exact copy of Napoleon, and the gray coat enveloping his thick-set figure increased the realistic effect.

Although he was evidently aware of this, and took pleasure in maintaining the pose, he did not lay himself open to ridicule: there was a threatening expression in his eyes, and his remarks were emphasized by the presence of the carbines at the door.

"Do you hear that?" he said, slowly; "there goes your last chance."

"It may be help coming," retorted Wallion imperturbably.

"Do you really think that?"

"You yourself need to study a map: you would be powerless against a well-planned surprise."

Ortiz raised his eyebrows, but his immediate reply virtually admitted the truth of the insinuation.

"A whole regiment would not be able to prevent my getting away by sea."

"As long as you did not fall in with two or three torpedo boats outside the headland!"

"Ah," murmured Ortiz, "is that why you sent off your friends?"

"Yes, they will give the alarm to the coast guards, if they have not already been warned. I had not counted on a stolen submarine when I came here, but now I know where I have you...."

As they talked, both men were on the alert for sounds from outside; people were approaching, and as though at a given signal, those inside the room re-grouped themselves.

Ortiz and Fayerling took a few quick steps towards the door, and the sentries grounded their rifles; Wallion, Raebel and Lona Ivanovna drew back towards the window, and stood in front of the pretended Andrei Bernin, in his armchair. The two groups kept a watchful eye on one another across the room.

"Discussion is useless," said Ortiz, presently; "your friends have failed —look!"

A confused mass of shadows became visible through the doorway, and rifle-butts clanged on the hall floor. Two weary and dejected figures were pushed forward into the circle of light in the middle of the room: they were Leo and Sonia, and Wallion could not repress an exclamation of disappointment.

"You have failed?" he said, going up close to Leo; "haven't you telephoned or done anything?"

The young man shook his head wearily:

"We did our best, but they were too clever for us: it was a trap."

In a few words he told his story. Sonia had taken refuge in her aunt's arms.

The journalist perceived that he could no longer expect help from any quarter, and that he must rely entirely upon his own skill and resourcefulness; it was like the final moves in a game of chess, when the board has been swept clean of all but a few pieces, and the antagonists are two evenly-matched and quick-witted players. Leo Grath and the others were pale with mortification: they had lost heart, and were powerless to make any further attempt to save themselves, though Max Raebel, who stood just behind the journalist, said in a low tone:

"We are out of our depth, Mr. Wallion, things look bad for us. But if you give the word, I am at your orders: at least, we can still use our fists!"

The journalist did not reply, but turned to Ortiz, who was listening to Rastakov's and Tassler's obsequious report.

"Gabriel Ortiz," he said quietly, "I warn you for the last time: we are under the protection of the law of Sweden."

The adventurer turned round, and inspected him from head to foot.

"I presume I am to consider that as a formal protest?"

"Yes. It is addressed to your friends as well as to yourself."

"My friends!" echoed Ortiz, in an indescribably contemptuous tone; "if I and my plans were dependent on my friends, I should be weaker than you. Do you suppose I take either friends or enemies into account? Your protest is futile, sir, and if you haven't perceived it already, I shall convince you of it."

He gave an order in Russian. The two marines stepped forward, and took possession of Lona Ivanovna's revolver, the butt of which was protruding from her workbag. The old Russian lady was taken off her guard, but she quickly realized that she was disarmed, and rapped out an indignant oath. Sonia caressed her soothingly:

"Never mind, Auntie," she whispered. "Keep still; don't make Sergius uneasy: he is looking this way, and I think he wants to say something to you."

"Yes, of course, child," murmured the old lady, irritably, "he wants to fight, and so do I; it is only natural…." She leaned across to the white-haired figure in the armchair, and a few brief sentences were exchanged between mother and son. The journalist watched her closely, for he feared that the hotheaded old Russian was contemplating some rash step, and suddenly he guessed that Sergius was still armed. Lona Ivanovna must be trying to persuade him to give her his revolver. Was she determined to make a fight for the document? To his relief, Sergius simply shook his head, and Lona Ivanovna drew back in high dudgeon. As she looked at Wallion, he said softly:

"Let sleeping dogs lie! Leave your son's revolver, we may need it later on."

The other marine now proceeded to search Wallion's clothes, turning over his papers, and rummaging in his pockets. He seemed greatly surprised at finding nothing, and called out something inquiringly. Ortiz waved his hand, and the man returned to the door. Wallion had allowed himself to be searched without saying a word, though he thought the more. The man had over-hauled him thoroughly and rapidly, and had probably been a policeman in former times: which would account for his dexterity. Ortiz had chosen his men carefully; supposing one of them had the inspiration to—no! The journalist resolutely banished that thought from his mind.

But some obscure association of ideas made him open his cigarette case, and light a cigarette at the tiny blue flame of the cigar-lighter which he always carried in his waistcoat pocket. A barely perceptible smile flitted across his face. Perhaps Ortiz noticed the smile, for he said in a harsh voice:

"You are unarmed; you have no possible means of communicating with the outer world; my will is paramount here: need I put things more plainly? My will! In those two words you have the only law that carries weight here tonight."

"And before what court of law will you enforce it?" inquired the journalist politely.

"Do you insist upon a set trial?"

"Oh, don't put yourself out on my account!"

"Take care! I am not accustomed to be spoken to in such a tone. I suppose you are trying to gain time? What can you hope for now? I assure you we could blow the Copper House into atoms tonight, without a single person being near enough to see even the reflection in the sky. Don't you hear that?"

Hear? Wallion *felt*, with every nerve in his body, the long-drawn out reverberations of the thunder-storm which raged anew over their heads, whilst the dark window-panes were continually lit up by the glare of the lightning. He knew perfectly well that the adventurer was not exaggerating.

"A court of law," Ortiz repeated. "Baron Fayerling, these people seem to expect us to perform a scene from comic opera!... Very good, if they are such sticklers for form, I appoint you as general prosecutor, baron, but be brief."

The baron said slowly:

"I accuse Maurice Wallion of having used force to hinder me in carrying out an appointed task, of having attacked my assistant Rastakov, and of having helped the thief, Bernard Jenin, to get away with Tarraschin's memorandum."

"A comprehensive indictment!" remarked Wallion.

"Do you deny it?"

"What would be the good?"

After a minute's silence, the baron proceeded:

"I accuse Lona Ivanovna, Andrei Ivanovitch, and Sonia Andreievna, of having received and hidden the thief, whose real name is Sergius Tassler."

"And whose father stands there!" interrupted Lona Ivanovna in a threatening voice, pointing at the merchant, who started back; "of what can *you* accuse your own son, and your former wife? Why are you silent? Are you beginning to feel what an utter worm you are, little Marcus? Speak, man! Out with it, or I am afraid you will choke...."

The merchant tried to reply, but his trembling lips could only articulate an indistinct murmur.

"Silence!" said Ortiz sharply.... "You are to answer and not to ask questions, Lona Ivanovna. Where have you hidden Sergius Tassler?" His dark, steadfast gaze seemed to read her inmost thoughts....

"You refuse to answer?"

He put his hands behind his back, and came up to her, thrusting out his head, and compelling her to meet his eyes.

"You are obstinate? Do you think I need your answer? I tell you, I saw through the whole of your miserable little secret as soon as I got into the room—but it amused me to play with you—look here!"

Before anyone guessed his intention, he had snatched the wig from the fugitive's head; the blue spectacles fell on the floor, and were broken. Sergius sprang up with a cry, and stood unmasked, pale and agitated before Ortiz, who continued with appalling composure:

"The game is up. No, my lad, your plan was really too audacious! You didn't calculate that I should be aware of the important fact that Andrei Bernin was dead; and besides, the man who wears a flowing beard on a young face, should be careful to keep in the dark....."

This revelation produced an overwhelming impression. The baron and Rastakov, realizing how they had been tricked, stood mute, glaring malignantly at the man who had foiled them; Lona Ivanovna tried to spring forward, but one of Rastakov's men pushed her back and raised his gun threateningly, whilst, as though in obedience to some preconcerted signal, four more armed men came in from the hall.

"Let him alone!" cried Lona Ivanovna. "I forbid you to touch him!"

Ortiz did not seem to hear her; without changing his position, he stood and studied Sergius Tassler's face, as though he were bent on solving a problem. Wallion, who in his turn, watched Ortiz narrowly and quietly, guessed what the problem was.

"So it was you who brought Tarraschin's memorandum out of Russia?" said the adventurer at length, thoughtfully. "What have you done with it?"

"I shall not tell you," replied Sergius vehemently; "what have you to do with us? We have a right...."

"I want no unnecessary explanations. I know all about you. Will you give me the paper of your own free will?"

"Never!"

"Then I shall take it."

"Don't be so sure that you can find it!"

"I have no need to search," replied Ortiz, raising his hand. "I don't think much of your intelligence: you are not wanting in brains, but you rely too much on yourself, and you lack imagination. You have hidden the paper somewhere about you—not in your clothes—they are liable to be searched, aren't they?—what else have you? Ah, give me your stick!"

A strange expression passed over Wallion's face, as Sergius mechanically held out his stick, and he could not restrain an audible "bravo," at the ingenuity of Ortiz' reasoning.

Ortiz turned round, with the stick in his hand:

"I appreciate your compliment, but the thing was perfectly simple. One could see from here that the handle of the stick unscrews. Meantime, your 'bravo' betrays that the secret was known to you, which makes it less likely that the paper is still in its hiding-place; indeed, it is hardly worth while looking inside."

He tossed the stick to the baron, who with nervous haste unscrewed the handle, and peeped into the cavity.

"Manifestly empty!" remarked Ortiz, coolly; "that was to be expected: it was a poor hiding-place, and no doubt you discovered it at once, Mr. Wallion?"

"Of course."

"You have it then?"

Wallion hesitated for the fractional part of a second.

"I can give you my word of honor that I have not removed the paper from the stick," he said then. "Are you so sure that it is not there after all?"

Leonard, who could not understand the journalist's intention, bit his lips; he was beginning to think that Wallion was altogether too complaisant, but Raebel gave him a dig in the ribs, and whispered with a smile:

"Have you ever seen an acrobat on the top of a pole? He's nothing to Wallion: just keep your eye on him. He's not the sort of man who comes to grief at the first round!"

Although the Austrian spoke lightly, the perspiration stood on his forehead: experience told him that the situation was critical, and he could see that Ortiz was getting to an end of his patience. He did not trouble further about the stick.

"Sergius Tassler," he said sharply, "if you wish to live you must answer me. Did you have Tarraschin's memorandum in your stick?"

Sergius started back a little, but made no reply; his dark, resigned face did not change, and he looked calmly at his tormentor.

"Answer him, for Heaven's sake," sobbed Sonia; "answer, Sergius, I won't have you die!"

His face softened at her passionate appeal, and he said curtly:

"I did hide the paper in my stick; I do not know who took it out; I have nothing further to say."

There was no mistaking his sincerity, and Ortiz showed no sign of doubting his word.

"You have said enough," he remarked, his eyes beginning to sparkle; "you have said more than enough, but you are even more imprudent than I thought: now I understand!"

His eyes rested for an instant on the young girl, with a thoughtful and not altogether unfriendly expression; then, with a shrug of the shoulders, he dismissed her from his mind, and for the first time turned his whole attention to Lona Ivanovna.

"It must be you," he accused her. "You are intelligent and determined: you said to yourself, 'It will be better for me to take the responsibility, Sergius is too weak.' You watched over your son at night, whilst he slept, didn't you? You need not answer: the thing is obvious; you took the document secretly, that you might hide it more securely. You felt yourself strong enough to bear the responsibility alone. Very good. The entire responsibility is yours, since you will have it so. Now you must answer me."

Lona Ivanovna replied steadily and unhesitatingly:

"Yes, I took it whilst Sergius was asleep. Only I know where it is to be found now—and you cannot frighten me!" She laughed grimly:

"I think I have baffled you this time. You may kill me, but you won't find what you are looking for. Those brutes have ransacked the whole house twice, and you may do it once again. You have no chance of succeeding, and you may believe that I know what I am saying, when you recollect that I have all my life been accustomed to play hide-and-seek with the Tsar's secret police. Go your way, Gabriel Ortiz, you have failed. An old woman has beaten you!"

The adventurer showed no sign of discomposure; he allowed her biting scorn to pass unobserved; not so her challenge.

After a few minutes' calculation, he said, more to himself than to her:

"There are only two or three places where you can have hidden it; but why waste time in guessing? There is a much simpler way."

As he said this, he showed his white, even teeth, not in a smile, but rather in the fixed grin of a wild beast, while a grim look came over his face, almost transforming its expression. He turned to the marines, and gave the word of command:

"Ready! The first to stir from his place will be shot."

Half a dozen rifle-muzzles were pointed at the prisoners.

"Rastakov, take your revolver and place it against Sergius Tassler's forehead. I will count three—and at the word 'three,' you will fire."

The six marines took careful aim, and nobody stirred, while Rastakov crossed the room, and placed his heavy weapon against Sergius' right temple. There was a breathless silence, for they all realized Ortiz' intention. Marcus Tassler turned ashen-gray; without a sound he left the room and was not seen again.

"I forbid anyone to stir a finger," Ortiz continued; "this business is between you and me, Lona Ivanovna. I have your son—you have the document: will you exchange?"

A dead pause ensued. The old lady raised her hand slowly to her throat, and gazed as though fascinated at Rastakov's forefinger, which was touching the trigger.

Sergius had closed his eyes.

"Don't think of me, Mother," he said, softly; "think only of our cause."

She opened her mouth, but no sound issued from her lips.

"One!"

Sonia sprang up, but Leo caught her in his arms, at a glance from the journalist, who was now very pale. Lona Ivanovna remained stiff and immovable.

"Let me go!" cried the girl, hysterically. "Oh, you—cowardly—wretches! If only I were a man!"

She sank down, half fainting, but weeping as though her heart would break. Wallion clenched his hands, but kept still; he seemed to be waiting for something.

"Two!"

A glazed look came over Lona Ivanovna's eyes, and she stared at Ortiz as though she had never seen him before; she seemed to look at him as though from an immense distance, and to be straining every nerve to control herself. She saw his pitiless eyes, his lips unclosing for the third time... she tore the workbag from her left arm, and threw it on the table.

"There!" she exclaimed. "Let Sergius go, you murderer! The paper is in the bag."

"In the bag!"

The adventurer put out his hand, but drew it quickly back.

"If you are lying, ..." he said threateningly.

"I am not lying," she replied wearily. "I took the paper out of the stick whilst Sergius was sleeping. I was certain that nobody would look for it in a place that was so apparent to everyone. The paper is very small, and in a tiny roll; it is lying amongst the lace-work.... Forgive me, Sergius!"

She sank down on a chair. Ortiz turned the bag upside down, and shook out the work on the table. Wallion was carefully choosing a cigarette from his case; he smiled: the matter was taking the turn for which he had hoped from the beginning, and Ortiz had already wasted nearly two precious hours; his own opportunity was come at last.

"Well, Gabriel Ortiz," said he, in a nonchalant tone, "is the memorandum there?"

The adventurer had searched all through the contents of the workbag; he now pushed it aside, and began to examine the folds of the lace with nervous eagerness.

"You won't find anything there," the journalist proceeded; "Lona Ivanovna made a mistake. The paper is not in her workbag: I have it!"

CHAPTER XIX

Wallion Speaks Out and
Rastakov Is Balked of His Prey

The journalist's utterly unforeseen announcement electrified everyone, and all faces were turned towards him, with intense surprise. That Maurice Wallion could have obtained possession of Tarraschin's memorandum, had occurred to none of them, least of all to Lona Ivanovna.

"You, you!" she stammered. "How is it possible?"

Ortiz' cold, hard voice broke in:

"Are you trying to shield her son? She is lying, the bag is empty—I do not believe you."

"Allow me to explain the situation," said the journalist, who still held in his left hand the cigarette which he had taken from his case, and, in his right the cigar-lighter, whose little flame burned clearly and evenly; his hands were perfectly steady.

"The paper really was in Lona Ivanovna's bag—until the time when, after hearing the story of the Bernin family, I demonstrated to them that the stick was empty, to Sergius Tassler's great astonishment. Following your example, Ortiz, I concluded that his mother, wishing to shift the responsibility on to her own shoulders, had secretly removed the paper, but, unlike you, I went a step further, and assumed, from what I knew of her character, that she had hidden it in her workbag, that well-known receptacle which everybody was accustomed to see hanging on her arm. I fully anticipated that you, my dear Ortiz, would proceed to the sort of compulsion we have just witnessed, and what would have been the good of her stratagem then? I at once decided to remove the precious document to its third, best, and final hiding-place. Under the pretext of examining Andrei Bernin's room, I was left alone with Lona Ivanovna for a few minutes, and—'hey presto!'— Russia's fate lay snugly in my waistcoat pocket. That is the story. You may conscientiously leave mother and son in peace, my dear Ortiz; the thief— that thief who caused the baron such heart-searchings—is none other than myself!"

"Damnation!" ejaculated Ortiz, his eyes bloodshot and staring; "shall I ever get hold of that infernal paper?"

"The outlook doesn't seem very promising," agreed the journalist, smiling. "It has passed through various hands in the last day or two, and its present owner—well, I have a pretty good idea that he will not let it out of his possession!"

His unshaken audacity took Ortiz aback: he hesitated for a minute, and the journalist availed himself of the pause.

"Let us talk things over," said he. "If anyone attempts to come near me, or to threaten me with his gun, I swear that you will never have the document."

"Where have you got it?" asked the adventurer reluctantly.

"Ah, where!" laughed Wallion. "One of your men searched me just now, didn't he? Did he find it? No. And yet I can assure you that he saw it. I believe he even touched it! You see this tiny flame, and this little cigarette? The moment I light my cigarette, your dreams for the future will vanish in smoke, Ortiz."

"You would pay dearly for it!"

"*You* would, you mean. A far too expensive cigarette, and that's a fact! Now, then, stand still, all the lot of you. Ortiz, keep them quiet. It wouldn't take me a second, and my death wouldn't be much of a compensation for your loss."

"I do not believe that Tarraschin's memorandum could be compressed into so small a space," Ortiz objected incredulously.

"Don't you?" returned the journalist. "Didn't Lona Ivanovna say that the paper was quite small, and tightly-rolled up? The idea struck me when I removed it from her bag, and just before you came, I made this arrangement, on the chance of my things being searched. You don't believe me? Look here, then."

He squeezed the little cylinder between his fingers, so that the cigarette paper burst, and fluttered to the ground, whilst a thin layer of tobacco fell from the ends; there remained in his hand a tightly rolled sheet of white paper, which began to uncurl as though a spring had been released. Ortiz leaned forward.

"No, keep back!" said the journalist. "You observe that the flame is all but touching the paper now. You can see perfectly well where you are—do you recognize Prince Tarraschin's handwriting? Shall I tell you that it is written in French? Shall I read it out to you?"

"You are mad!" muttered Ortiz hoarsely. "What can you do? If you leave this room, you will be shot."

"Yes, from behind, I suspect. But I prefer to stop here, I have something to say to you…."

"If you stay here with that paper in your hands, you will be shot. You have never been in greater danger than you are now."

"I'm not so sure of that! Have you really the moral courage to watch Tarraschin's document burn? Make up your mind, I am waiting."

Ortiz watched the journalist's movements like a lynx, but Wallion had gauged him correctly: he could not bring himself to run the risk, however willingly he would have given the order to shoot the man who was daring to thwart him on the very threshold of success. He gave a reluctant signal, and the weapons were lowered.

"Speak out!" he said, "what do you want?"

Wallion stepped back a few paces. His bold "coup" had made him master of the situation for the time being, but the outlook was dangerous in the extreme. He must keep an eye on practically all his enemies at once: should but one of them succeed in raising his gun, he would be lost; he was a prisoner, and compelled to plan his escape as best he could, alone and unarmed, under the eyes of his captors. Speed was all-important; never had he felt his mind clearer or cooler than now, as he reviewed every possibility. He knew that Sergius Tassler had a revolver within reach, hidden presumably among the rugs of his armchair: and he remembered that Max Raebel only awaited a signal to come to his assistance: on these two facts, his entire scheme must be built up.

"Order Rastakov to stand back," he said briefly; "Sergius Tassler has nothing more to do with this case."

The Russian had remained standing near Sergius, but at a nod from his employer, he thrust his revolver back into his pocket, and returned to his place by the door. As he did so, Wallion exchanged a rapid glance with the Austrian. He saw Raebel's intelligent eyes widen inquiringly, and he nodded almost imperceptibly. The Austrian understood the signal, and would now be ready to play his part; Wallion relied implicitly upon his experience and ready wit. The important thing now, was to engross Ortiz' whole attention for the next few minutes, and the journalist began again with a laugh:

"Yes, I have something to say to you, Ortiz; this is a good opportunity, for I am afraid we shall not meet again after tonight. You intend to kill me, if you can; I intend to render you harmless, if I can: the situation is not without its piquancy."

Ortiz had pulled out his handkerchief and was drying his hands nervously: there was little of the Great Napoleon about his strained features at this moment.

"You talk too much," he said hoarsely; "get to business."

"By all means. Your line has run out, my dear Ortiz. There was a time when I admired you, in spite of my position as your natural enemy. Your former adventures attracted me by a sort of simple and great-hearted freshness which characterized them, but the gigantic plan which is now dragging you to the verge of a precipice, is marked by an arrogance which the gods might envy. I can no longer admire a man who allows murder and robbery to be the milestones on his road to success; you should have kept your hands clean, Ortiz: there is too much blood on them! All the millions which you have distributed so lavishly, cannot alter the fact that you are a murderer, at war with Society, and, there, self-condemned."

The adventurer glared angrily at him, and exclaimed:

"I do not expect you to understand me! You and I stand at opposite ends of the great, unimpressionable fabric of Society; how could you enter into my plans and my dreams?"

The journalist did not reply immediately. He had seen Max Raebel move a shade closer to Sergius Tassler, and exchange two or three words with him, and a suppressed excitement began to rise in him, as he continued:

"Is your plan so difficult to fathom? You forget that I have read Tarraschin's memorandum, that I know what has become of your millions, and that I am well aware of the snare of specious promises in which you have entangled your dupes. You are not so strong as you imagine; you have worked to overthrow one party, and to support the other, so that you might use the gratitude of the successful one as a stepping-stone to power. But the Russian Revolution in March was none of your doing: you made a start in the opposite direction, and threw in your lot with the reactionaries, whose prospects seemed the more favorable. You made a mistake there: Kerensky still sits firmly in the saddle, and Prince Tarraschin's promises will never be fulfilled, for however strong your followers may be, they will never restore the Tsar to power."

He spoke slowly and impressively, and his words were now addressed to the silent group by the door, rather than to their leader. He noticed a strange expression in Rastakov's black eyes.

Perhaps Ortiz saw it too, for he exclaimed furiously:

"Silence! You lie!"

"Shall I give you a summary of Tarraschin's written promises?" returned Wallion, calmly, and, as Ortiz did not answer, he continued:

"To be called 'Emperor of the Amazons' was, after all, a barren honor; but as Governor-General of Siberia, you would rule over one of the largest countries in the world. Can you deny that Prince Tarraschin promised that post to you, on behalf of his party?"

A murmur went round the room, and Rastakov's face wore a threatening look, as he took in the full meaning of Wallion's information. Ortiz fathomed his enemy's intention, and grew pale; it almost seemed that his iron will was shaken, but he controlled himself with a tremendous effort, and said:

"You have read it yourself, and hold the proof of it in your hand. I have never hesitated, and I do not hesitate now; but if you imagine that my fate depends on a paper, you deceive yourself. I have many strings to my bow. Governor-General of Siberia?—let that pass, as you have said it, but it would only be a beginning: the whirlpool is deep, I can subdue it." He raised his voice, and turned to the silent audience round the door.

"Have I not proved to you that I keep my promises? Has your future ever looked so bright as it does now? I tell you, I can give you all that your wildest dreams can picture. Power or riches, you have only to choose; I have them both at my command."

He chose his words cleverly, on the spur of the moment, and Wallion realized that it was not only his millions that had attracted scores of adherents to his cause. His personal strength fascinated them, and his convincing arguments overruled their judgment. But the journalist had no intention of allowing him time to vindicate himself. He gathered that Max Raebel had by this time succeeded in conveying some sort of brief, but evidently reinspiring intimation to Leonard Grath, Sonia, and Lona Ivanovna in turn, for their faces had brightened with an expression of eager anticipation. A moment later, seeing that Ortiz' attention was temporarily diverted, the Austrian looked significantly from Wallion to the two lamps. The journalist understood his meaning, and nodded: it was nearly time!

"Do not promise more than you can perform, Ortiz!" he exclaimed. "What about those earlier promises of yours? Did you not assure Rastakov and his people that the Bolshevists are your friends? You, the organizer of the Reactionary Party in Russia?—for shame, what duplicity! What about these last Bolshevist uprisings in Petrograd? Were they your work?"

The vehemence of Wallion's attack struck Ortiz dumb.

"I… I am not obliged to answer," he said after a pause; "you are not my judge!"

"But you would like to be mine, wouldn't you? Perhaps you would rather I burned the document?"

The paper hovered nearer the little blue flame, and Ortiz exclaimed:

"Name your own price!"

It was a sign of weakening: he was ready to buy what he could not take by force.

Wallion laughed, feigning intense surprise:

"Is this little flame so valuable? You would see it extinguished at any price?"

"I will give you ten millions if you will blow it out," sad the adventurer. "And your liberty…."

"A fantastic offer!" said Wallion, his eyes glittering. "Does the future Governor of Siberia propose it?"

"Yes."

"Well, I decline it. You are a beaten man, Ortiz. Kerensky's government has suppressed the Bolshevist risings in Petrograd, and remains in power till further notice. A reactionary rising would be even less successful...."

Hardly had the journalist completed his sentence, when a dramatic interruption occurred.

Rastakov sprang forward. All the savagery in his primitive nature had risen to the surface, his face was convulsed, and his voice like the snarl of some wild beast:

"Is it true that the Bolshevists are beaten?" he cried.

"Yes; did you not know it?" answered Wallion.

"No! I thought... Ortiz, you have played us false! Remember what you promised!"

Ortiz struck him full in the face.

"How dare you, Rastakov!" he exclaimed harshly. "I have not paid you to insult me."

The blow left a red mark on Rastakov's white face. He staggered back, his hands clutching the air; his eyes looked like those of a blind man.

"Traitor!" he yelled.

Slipping his right hand into his pocket, he raised it high over his head, grasping a round, black object, which he was about to fling at Ortiz, when the baron, throwing his whole weight upon him, wrenched the deadly thing away, and dashed it through the nearest window, far out into the park.

The whole house was shaken by a terrific explosion, a column of earth and flame rose high into the air, for a minute, and the atmospheric pressure drove in the window-panes with a clatter of breaking glass.

Before the last splinters had fallen on the carpet, Ortiz drew a revolver from his pocket, and, apparently without even taking aim, shot Rastakov through the head. The unfortunate Russian fell where he stood, and did not move again.

Rastakov was balked of his prey, and had paid for his mistake with his life.

The sudden tragedy paralyzed them all. Ortiz stared down at the dead body.

"One more!" he muttered; "one more!"

At that minute, the journalist made an alarming discovery; the draught from the broken window had blown out the little flame in the cigar-lighter. There was not an instant to lose!

"Now, Raebel!" he cried, and crouched down as quick as lightning. The Austrian thrust his hand among the rugs on Sergius Tassler's armchair, and pulled out a bright steel "Browning," which he aimed at the lamps. Two shots rang out, and the lamps fell crashing to the floor.

The room was plunged in darkness.

CHAPTER XX

In Which Wallion Shows That a Great Deal Can Be Done in Ten Minutes

It seemed as though a black velvet pall had been dropped over them. The sudden transition from brilliant light to impenetrable darkness, was almost physically painful, and ten or fifteen seconds passed before anyone attempted to stir; each man was listening with bated breath for his enemy's movements. A flash pierced the darkness: Ortiz had fired at the journalist, or rather, at the spot where he had last seen him standing. An infernal hubbub broke out: someone turned on an electric torch, which was immediately shattered by a shot; a dozen rifles rang out simultaneously, furniture fell to the ground, and panes of glass jingled.

"Get lights!" cried Ortiz, imperiously; "let no one escape: stand by the windows and doors!"

The journalist had carefully placed Tarraschin's memorandum in his pocket-book and was now ready to avail himself of the opportunity; he moved noiselessly forward, and suddenly threw himself into the tumult round the door. Striking out to right and left, his broad shoulders soon cleared him a passage. A last shot was fired almost under his chin, and he found himself out in the hall—free!

There was no time to lose. The hall was dark, but the tramp of feet warned him that at least half a score of men were making their way through the glass doors. That way was obviously impossible. Towards the kitchen regions, a faint light could be seen through the half-open door: that exit was blocked too; to reach the upper floor by the staircase, was his only chance. He hastened in that direction, blessing the thick carpet, which deadened his footsteps, and took the twenty-five stairs in four bounds. As he gained the topmost stair, he dropped down on the landing like a cat, and held his breath: he had heard someone breathing close by. But in a moment he uttered a sigh of relief, as a familiar voice said softly:

"It is I, Max Raebel. I know your step again, Wallion; this way!"

He discerned a shadowy form, and a hand grasped his.

"I think we may congratulate ourselves that we have won the first round," added the Austrian.

"What about the others?"

"Oh, I told Sergius Tassler and Grath to see to the ladies; I advised them to offer no resistance, but if possible to take refuge in the gardener's cottage. Ortiz will concentrate his attention on us."

"It looks like it," Wallion agreed.

The hall beneath them was filled with light. Fresh lamps had been brought in and lighted, but a strange condition of uncertainty seemed to prevail, and two or three voices were clamoring for Rastakov. Baron Fayerling hurried forward, and the six marines marched across the hall towards the stairs, with Ortiz behind them. At sight of him, the threatening murmurs died away, and with a few decided orders the baron quelled the disturbance.

"The harmony seems slightly defective!" whispered the Austrian, "but it will soon be too hot for us here; which way shall we go?"

"To the winding-staircase on the back landing," replied Wallion promptly. They crossed the passage, and he opened the door leading to the backstairs, but immediately retreated, and bolted it hastily; he had almost run into the arms of three of the forest-guards, who were evidently on the look-out for him, and now began to batter on the door.

"The deuce!" he murmured, "this is what one may call quick work! Back again!"

They ran back to the main staircase, which was now their only chance, if they were not to be caught on that floor.

"Are you armed?" asked Raebel.

"No, are you?"

"Yes, I have Sergius Tassler's revolver, but only four cartridges left."

Ortiz' bodyguard had nearly reached the top, when the two detectives appeared on the landing. A shout greeted them, but before anyone could shoot, the fugitives had gained the second floor, where Raebel turned and fired a shot down the stairs.

"That'll just give them something to think about," he explained; "I am generous, as long as I have anything to give away."

"That leaves you with only three shots, doesn't it?" said Wallion. "Wait, that is not enough; I must get hold of something for myself also."

They heard someone running up, and the journalist stood a little to one side. One of the marines, more quick-footed than the rest, appeared at the top of the stairs. Wallion sprang silently upon him, seized him by the back of the neck, swung him round, wrested the carbine from the hands of the surprised and bewildered man, and, with a violent push, sent him reeling backwards down the stairs. The living projectile evidently landed in the very midst of his advancing comrades, and a chorus of shouts and execra-tions followed. Wallion examined the carbine, which was loaded with five rounds of ammunition.

"Come along," said he, "we can't stop here."

They mounted the third flight, which was narrower, and led straight to the attics, and they looked round them in the darkness. Every corner was filled with dusty boxes, worn-out furniture, and a medley of nondescript objects; on the far side, they made out a ladder, set up against the ceiling, beneath a bolted trapdoor. Wallion struck a match, and looked at his watch: it was half-past nine. Their pursuers came on noisily, though rather out of breath. Raebel seized an old high-backed oak armchair, swung it up over his head, and hurled it with a crash down the attic-stairs. A shot answered the challenge, and a bullet whistled past the Austrian's right ear, as he stepped back swearing softly:

"There's no stopping them," he grumbled; "a machine-gun is what we want!"

The journalist was already at the top of the ladder, and pushing up the creaking trapdoor. The Austrian followed him, and they both crawled out upon the sloping copper roof. The night air blew cool and refreshing on their heated faces, and Wallion let the heavy trapdoor fall back into its place.

"Shall we stop here," asked Raebel eagerly. "We could give them a warm reception from this position."

Wallion considered.

"No," he said; "we have too little ammunition, and besides, there are several attic windows from which they might fire on us."

"But where in the world can we go?" exclaimed the flabbergasted Raebel. "It seems to me, we have come as far as we can without flying!"

"Follow me: I have an idea."

The journalist turned, and began to creep along the roof, which was wet and slippery. The rain had ceased, and the thunder no longer rumbled, but the sky was still overcast, and the darkness denser than ever. Raebel was no coward, but he was beginning to find the situation far from pleasant, and muttered wrathfully to himself.

"Be careful here," the journalist's voice warned him; "it's a curb roof, as you know, and slopes abruptly."

"Where are you going?" asked Raebel.

"I am crawling down to the eaves," explained Wallion, his voice seem-ing to come unexpectedly from beneath the Austrian's feet. He followed his companion's example, slid dizzily down, and fortunately brought up, feet foremost, at the eaves. There, to his indescribable horror, he heard an extraordinary creaking and crashing, out in the empty space beyond the edge of the roof.

"Where are you, Wallion?" he faltered.

"Here," replied a calm voice. "Don't you remember the old oak tree behind the house? Spring right out from where you are now, and you will find it is almost like jumping on to a mattress."

"Gracious Heaven!" thought the Austrian, shutting his eyes, and without waiting for any miracle from above, he took the leap, just as two carbines were fired through the trapdoor.

It seemed an age before he fell into a network of yielding branches. Wallion's hand grasped him, and he found himself sitting astride a good-sized bough.

"A bird couldn't have done it better," whispered his friend. "This is a funny life, but at any rate, we are making them dance to our tune!"

"And where next?" inquired Raebel faintly.

"Down to terra firma again, of course!"

They climbed down, and reached the ground breathless, but unhurt. A loud shout was heard on the roof, and a shot was fired in reply from the terrace.

"We must get right away from the house!" cried Wallion; "there's just one chance in ten that we may find the coast clear."

They ran helter-skelter through the nearest bushes, and came out on the open space in front of the stable and cowhouse. But they had not gone ten steps, before lights began to twinkle on all sides, and they saw dark figures hurrying to intercept them.

"No," said Raebel, "not one chance in a thousand. It is not within human power to shake them off: they are worse than teazles!"

Both men felt that they were not up to a long chase, exhausted as they were after their efforts, and they instinctively steered their course towards the stable, rushed in, and fastened the massive bolt. Here they would at least gain a moment's respite, though they could hear the steps of their pursuers outside, surrounding the building. They breathed more easily, and looked at each other by the light of a match.

"Listen," said Wallion slowly. "If help doesn't come soon, we shall both be done for; we have seen too much, and Tarraschin's memorandum is in my pocket-book. The document is all-important. If either of us can save it, well and good: but if the worst happens, it must be destroyed. Agreed?"

"Agreed!" replied Raebel, seriously.

They shook hands. A bullet crashed through the door. The match went out, but Wallion struck another. The two horses in the stalls turned their heads uneasily, and blinked at them with great, solemn eyes. They passed through the stable, climbed into the hay-loft, and pulled the ladder up after them. A minute later, the stable door was burst open by a powerful blow from a huge piece of timber, and the place was invaded by a swarm of dark figures. Wallion and Raebel fired simultaneously, and a cry betrayed that someone had been hit; the besiegers drew back a little, and there was a pause which lasted for several minutes.

"That was too risky for them," whispered the Austrian; "they are evidently meditating something else, but what?"

The silence made him uneasy.

"I don't like this," he murmured. "Why haven't they returned?"

Wallion said nothing. They could hear steps outside, voices, strange noises of different kinds. A shout was heard in the distance. Suddenly a heavy body fell upon the tiled roof, which was splintered by the blow, something fell with a thud into the hay, and lay hissing close to them. Wallion sprang up.

"Fire!" he shouted.

A violent explosion flung him against the wall, and a tongue of flame shot up through the hole in the roof. The hay had caught fire and was beginning to burn with a dark, smoky blaze, which spread rapidly, filling the loft with light, and making it intensely hot. In their first bewilderment, Wallion and Raebel stood irresolute.

"The swine!" exclaimed the Austrian indignantly. "The treacherous brutes!"

He would have tried to drop the ladder again through the trapdoor, but a bale of burning hay fell into the aperture and blocked it. He staggered back, shielding his face with his hands.

"Shut in!" he said bitterly; "trapped like rats!"

They retreated before the fire to the other end of the loft, where there was still one portion which the flames had not reached, since there was no hay in that half of the building. The journalist looked at his watch, and the Austrian, irritated at the meaningless precision of the action, exclaimed:

"That's right, I suppose you are going to make a note of the exact instant of our death!"

"It is just ten o'clock," replied Wallion deliberately. Over their heads, the tiles on the roof were cracking from the heat, with a noise like the rattle of rifle-practice; the fire was speedily consuming the woodwork, the roof-joists were burning, and the floor itself began to give way.

They heard the terrified horses break loose, and gallop away, neighing wildly. The two men were now the only living creatures left in the burning stable.

Then the journalist went up to the great double trap-doors, which were only opened to hoist up the bales of hay, and, as though to get air, he unbarred them and threw them wide open. A loud shout greeted his appearance, as his tall figure was unexpectedly outlined against the glare of the fire. He looked down into the darkness, and became aware of a crowd of upturned faces, and gleaming rifle-barrels.

"Is Ortiz there?" he called out.

The adventurer stepped slowly to the front, his hands behind his back in his favorite attitude.

"What do you want?" he asked. "Have you made up your mind to surrender?"

"No, I only want to remind you that I still have the Tarraschin memorandum, and it will not be much to your advantage to burn me alive."

"What do you expect me to do, then? I should be no better off if I shot you on the spot. The decision lies with you: give me the paper, and you are free."

The journalist seemed scarcely to hear him. A look of intense excitement had come into his eyes, which were fixed on the wooded ridge near the house, and a sigh of relief burst from him as he saw a white light flash out once.

"No, my dear Ortiz, I am not going to give you the document, but, on the contrary, this!" he cried, and raising his carbine he fired three successive shots into the darkness. Ortiz sprang back.

"What do you mean?" he exclaimed.

A rocket shot up from the bay, and burst in ten thousand stars. Frantic whistles were heard from the Copper House, together with an extraordinary medley of voices, knockings, shots and running feet.

"Go and see what is happening!" ordered Ortiz.

"Do not trouble, for I can tell you," said Wallion. "It is what I have been waiting for the whole of this long evening; it is my lieutenant, Robert Lang, who has come with the police."

Ortiz did not stir, but his very soul seemed to look out of his eyes, as he fixed them on his enemy.

"Were you clever enough for that after all?" said he. "I could not have believed it. I admit that I have underrated your powers. I suppose you think you have trapped me now?"

"That I cannot say: but I do know one thing, Ortiz: this is the end of your glorious dream!"

The adventurer seized a rifle, and fired at the black silhouette of the man who had outwitted him.

"You shall not survive it!" he shouted. "Farewell, Wallion!"

The journalist staggered back, and fell on to the floor. A loud voice was calling from some way off:

"The police! Where is the Chief? The police are here!"

CHAPTER XXI

The End of a Glorious Dream

The stampede began. Two minutes after the alarm had been given, not a man was left near the stable, which was now burning on every side, casting a vivid radiance over its immediate neighborhood. It struck them later as extraordinary that the gang had retreated without a single attempt at resistance. The last shot was that fired by Ortiz himself, and aimed at his bitterest foe—Maurice Wallion. From that hour, nobody set eyes upon the reincarnated Napoleon; it is to be supposed that, like his great prototype after the defeat at Waterloo, he apathetically allowed himself to be hurried away by his panic-stricken followers. He was hopelessly beaten, he had lost everything, and he must have realized this: he chose to vanish into the night....

Wallion had not been hit. Together with Raebel he jumped down from the granary, the floor of which collapsed a minute later.

"That's what one may call a rescue at the eleventh hour!" exclaimed the Austrian. "But what puzzles me is how did help come, when we had been unable to send a word of our plight?"

"I was prepared for the worst this morning," answered Wallion; "Robert Lang had orders to come to our relief on the stroke of ten, if he had heard nothing from me by then. The reason why I was so anxious to send him a message, is very simple: the submarine, of course, necessitated special measures, and I am afraid that Lang has omitted to take them."

This simple explanation made the Austrian open his eyes; he gave a prolonged whistle of admiration, and said:

"Wallion, you're an out-and-outer!"

Policemen, in plain clothes and in uniform, now began to spread round the Copper House in a wide semi-circle, and they went to meet them. Robert Lang was at the head, with several police officers of higher grade.

"Hallo, Lang!" cried Wallion. "You are punctual, thank goodness, but tell me quickly, how things stand as regards the channel into the bay?"

The young man stood still.

"The channel into the bay?" he echoed.

"Yes. Have you a patrol-boat outside?"

"No. Is that necessary?"

Raebel threw up his hands at this question, and exclaimed:

"Then Ortiz will get away!"

Wallion briefly explained the situation. The news of the submarine created a sensation, and one of the policemen hurried off to alarm the coast guard. After an instant's hesitation, the main body of police resumed their march to the sea-shore. Not a light was to be seen in the bay, but suddenly the noise of an engine was heard through the damp, still atmosphere, and a strange, dark mass became visible in the channel between the island and the shore. It was the submarine, towing the lighter after it. The deck of the latter was crowded with men; a gloomy silence reigned on board, and the ports of the submarine were closed.

Lona Ivanovna came running, followed by Sergius, Sonia and Leo. The last-named wrung the journalist's hand, in silent gratitude, but the old Russian exclaimed:

"What are you doing, Mr. Wallion? You're not allowing Ortiz to escape!"

The journalist replied, thoughtfully:

"He can't escape from himself."

She did not understand him.

"And Tarraschin's memorandum?" she asked.

"We'll talk of that by and by. I have it quite safe."

On board the lighter, the clanking of machinery became audible, and the tow-line was cast loose. The submarine shot away, and steered for the open sea, leaving a white trail of foam in its wake. The spectators began to run along the beach, and came out on the little promontory. On land, the police had completed their "round-up," which yielded a harvest of fourteen abandoned, dejected individuals, all captured unarmed, and asserting their innocence. But it looked as though their Chief was to get away in spite of everything. Wallion stood on the furthest point, looking out to sea.

"Fog!" he remarked, laconically.

A dense, gray wall was rising out of the Baltic, and driving in towards the land. The submarine continued to steer east at full speed, leaving the lighter to shift for itself; both entered the fog-belt, and disappeared.

Robert Lang reproached himself bitterly for his remissness, but Wallion said:

"You couldn't have known it, and besides, what matter if he slips through our fingers for the time being? He has nothing left to hope for...."

He spoke in a low tone, and without shifting his gaze from the sea. Was he waiting for something?

Ten minutes passed. Then the sea of fog was tinged with a sudden crimson glow, which seemed to come from a point due east of the outlying islands. A deafening and prolonged explosion rent the air; then darkness settled down again, and silence reigned once more over the sea. They looked at one another.

"A mine-explosion?" suggested someone.

"The submarine!" cried Robert Lang. "It came from that direction. A catastrophe must have occurred on board."

"Or—something else!" said Wallion. "Ortiz went on board as a defeated man:—and Rastakov's comrades...."

He bent his head and turned away.

"It is late. Let us go."

* * * *

Two days later, quite a little company was assembled in Lawyer Burchardt's office. There were Leonard Grath, Lona Ivanovna, Sonia and Sergius. The lawyer trotted up and down his sunny room, and looked incessantly at the clock. All faces were cheerful and free from anxiety, but a certain solemnity pervaded the atmosphere, and nobody seemed inclined to talk. Twelve o'clock struck, and the lawyer stopped his pacing, and looked expectantly at the door.

It opened, and admitted Maurice Wallion in travelling costume.

"Good morning," he said, with a smile. "I have to go abroad this afternoon, so you must excuse me if I seem a little hurried."

He shook hands with everybody, and gave Leo a small packet, saying as he did so:

"Take back your property; it is an atonement from a man who is sincerely repentant."

The young man opened the parcel, and colored with astonishment.

"The mortgages on the Copper House!" he exclaimed.

"Yes," answered the journalist, smiling. "Take them, you deserve a reward after all you have gone through, but ask no questions."

He turned to Lona Ivanovna.

"I have a message for you. You know that Marcus Tassler quitted the Copper House when Ortiz threatened your son's life. From that minute, he became another man, and fled from Ortiz' neighborhood, never to return. He wishes me to tell you that he regrets the past, and that you will never see him again."

The old Russian lady appeared deeply moved.

"Did you go and look for him?"

"Yes, I have had a talk with him."

"And—you let him go?"

"Yes, he is broken and changed. We must be merciful…."

The old lady bowed.

"I thank you," she said simply.

"I have another very important piece of news for you," Wallion continued. "Raebel and I, with the help of certain interested persons in various quarters, have settled the question of Tarraschin's memorandum, which is now in the hands of its rightful owner. Yes, Sergius Tassler, you must forgive me, but you know you had really no right to it at all! You shall not be a loser in the matter. I am authorized to inform the Bernin family that they are at liberty to return to Russia."

He smilingly deprecated their delighted expressions of gratitude, and continued:

"This brings the whole matter to a definite conclusion. Gabriel Ortiz' gigantic 'coup' has failed, and he himself has vanished without leaving any trace. I suppose you have seen the notices in the newspapers about the mysterious mine-explosion? That's the end of a many-sided adventure. By special request from an influential quarter, no official report will be published. The fourteen men who were arrested will be deported. Whatever the future holds, my friends, none of you will ever hear anything more of Gabriel Ortiz."

He was silent for a little.

"He was a man, after all!" he added, but he saw that none of them quite understood him. Sonia had clasped Sergius' hand, and regardless of them all, was pressing it to her cheek. Wallion bowed gallantly to her.

"I wish you a happier and brighter future," he said, smiling; "you are worthy of it!"

With these words, he left the room, and they looked after him with a pang of regret in the midst of their happiness, for they felt that they were losing a friend, and that his path might never again cross their own.

* * * *

A letter from Maurice Wallion to the Author, dated Montreal, July 20th, 1918.

"My dear Author,

"I suppose it must be! Tell what happened at the Copper House in your own way: of course, there will be more fiction than fact, but that can't be helped!

"You can say that I was mistaken as I have never been mistaken before (except in the case of Madame Lorette Chandeloup, whose story I will tell you some day). I believed that Gabriel Otiz could be conquered, and I was wrong. The man died unconquered. I salute his memory: I could have wished to be his friend.

"Don't forget to lay stress upon one thing: that two important points in this mad adventure have never been cleared up. First, what became of all that was left of Ortiz' millions? They disappeared, as though by magic, from the banks, between the 10th and 20th of July, 1917. The Whirlpool engulfed them. I know that Marcus Tassler did not embezzle them, and it is a mystery to me what became of them.

"The second point is: is Gabriel Ortiz really dead? What actually happened that night out in the Baltic? That red glare haunts me!

"You know that Russia is still suffering. Kerensky's fall soon succeeded that of Ortiz: neither of them was strong enough to steer the drifting ship, which still awaits its master-pilot. Bolsheviks, Czecho-Slovaks, monarchists, and foreign powers are injuring themselves without gaining one atom of honor or happiness in exchange for all the blood they are shedding. Is Ortiz still behind the scenes? Has he risen from his grave to play the 'grand jeu'? I cannot tell. You may say: after all, he was only a grain of dust in the whirlpool. Possibly. Has not a grain of dust been able to change the course of the world before now?

"It is just a year today since I fought him at the Copper House for Tarraschin's memorandum. Somehow I feel that I shall see him again: I would stake my life on it!

"Good-bye, and, perhaps, 'au revoir'!

"In haste, between two adventures,

"Yours very sincerely,
"Maurice Wallion."

www.ingramcontent.com/pod-product-compliance
Lightning Source LLC
Chambersburg PA
CBHW011446170626
46816CB00008B/2544